THE KEPT ECCLESIA OF Agatha Moi

ELIZABETH CLAYTON

Brilliant Books Literary
137 Forest Park Lane Thomasville
North Carolina 27360 USA

CONTENTS

Acknowledgments 5

Preface Impromptu 7

Preface.. 9

Related Afterthought.. 17

Portions... 19

Introduction.. 21

Agatha, Moi 23

the *Ecclesia*, Opened 25

Sayings 27

Parables/Riddles 35

Lines 53

Verses 99

Conclusion.. 179

Conclusive Aside 183

About the Author 189

ACKNOWLEDGMENTS

Acknowledgment remarks are in one sense, paradoxical: they are, with necessary discretion, brief, but in sentiment very full. A number of friends and colleagues have helped with this work—for their interest and efforts, I am most appreciative—and most, supporting the preparation of the entire finished manuscript, faithful Ora Steele who has seen, with me, the project into completion—more roses Ora, a lovely addition to your already full bouquet.

PREFACE IMPROMPTU

Agatha Moi is a long-thought, very full bramble of ruminations of a life through which struggle enabled the sacrament of a kind of purification—a cleanliness of negativism, fear, and doubt, the redressing of fear, and the pathos of understanding the loss of, most, beauty—into an acceptance of an argument aspiring which became, finally, truly unnecessary. The mind, consciousness— reason—searches always for order so that it can function properly; unfortunately, in many matters of the heart, "reason does not comply." And if it were to do so, it would not offer the result of gain. We are mortals with inner seams of the celestial, and we must wear these both together.

"Wearing" can prove difficult, as the verse narrative demonstrates, but using its reality of studied perception with the "forward appendage of thought"—hope—a cathartic quest has offered a medium, a fashion after the grail: one of truths, beauty, and acceptance without regret.

Pleasing others is a maneuver we humans use to assure ourselves that we can then accept our own behavior, be counted worthy within, and safe. Agatha does not conclude until late that her very own perceptions may not have been that often adverse, at least in many instances, to those of others. Of a pressing strength, not truly disclosed, perhaps energy rising out intense doubt against hope—and its accompanying, frustrations, anger, and such—of self, she chose to say what could not be contained, and as the narrative concludes, "stars dress (her) person," so that she does not need to continue to struggle to reach "for the sun and moon."

If wisdom be found through example, perhaps we may look into ourselves to accept and trust, if with questions, the spirit waiting there to be unveiled, to not be in reactive discovery, challenged, or filled of questions yet thought found unworthy. Growth can occur within the rooms of doubt, like examination: casting off reaffirming or finding new alternatives, but we must be wise in the thoughtful simplicity of a behavior truly no more than rearranging—replacing an acceptable portion of truth in the portion left empty—that we not be found "left waiting," without our "stars" to dress our "person."

PREFACE

In the vastness of the number indicating the grande coming of years, which has passed over our cosmos, the sum of the ages, and eons would be too great for our full comprehension. We can, yet, hardly conceptualize ancient man and his world. But in many ways, we are similar or almost so, in numerous behaviors. We were conceived and born alike and have and will depart the earth in death. However, changes began with the first man, and throughout history, recorded in written or oral form, steps occurred, at times large, with small within—almost as a wave of searching humanity—so that we are in our places today: the marvelous discovery of the thumb, fire, weapons; the great flood and navigation into living in groups, shelters, cities, and states alongside cultivation of seeds and medicinal agents, having yet the passion left over to create work which we yet admire.

Ancient man not only evolved physically to, at first, survive, but his mental faculties progressed also. He learned, if more slowly, of his world within as without: fear, courage, brotherhood, and honor—and he learned of a need for the embodiment of the small spark inside himself—and so we see the development of the construct of divinity, the I-thou relationship. God remained the center of the universe until the beginning years of the Renaissance when, out the ideology of the new "humanism," man became the center, and so remains today.

The years, decades, centuries, continued constant, true, with the "waves," movements, transitions—steps and steps: the four great religions came into civilized portions of the entire globe, the pastoral became secondary to the great industrial revolution and personal philosophies were greatly in flux; men now wanted to live, work, and be safe, but in more comfort and esteem. A sameness among the all was in the offing, and boundaries, almost unseen, began to fall to small particulars so that the physical self came into conflict with the advancing psychological self, and we are almost home in this recantation.

The developing self/soul has grown to dimensions almost too great to measure for they are not physical mass but, descriptively, energy in thought processes, the growth facilitated by communication, that rare and select between one and another: closeness to another allows more completely the reflection it supplies, and we have the strength of two in one:

Celestial airs,
Thy breathing comes to me, of life in one of two—

There is, then, the rather formidable matter of self-disclosure and could be, perhaps looked upon by the pensive mind as the complete center of the self; it is not, at all, in any great awareness but is reflected in very obvious ways: in appointments of homes, vehicles, vocations, political and spiritual affiliations; myriads of behaviors, different and similar, are exhibited in patterns that reflect both conscious and unconscious motivation toward disclosure needs.

It may be that disclosure is central to our behavior because it comes with the breath of life—our separation from our safe, organic Eden, one from which we are never truly free, preluded by violent thrusting/ entering an environment which very early demands effort toward some kind of control; with this circumstance in place, we search all of our lives, in passive or more aggressive manner, in absurd and perverted routines, to find a "oneness" that can help make us wholly safe again in the sharing—an inevitable grail, this sentiment beautifully expressed by the ancient dervish poet, Rumi:

Remember those in prison here in separation's night;

Many do find their bliss, but probably, when reading current statistics and trends, projections—and observing one's own culture, and others'—apparently, most do not. Weltanschauungs offer, always, different steps from which to choose and, in addition one or several of many "recipes." schedules, patterns we may grow into, plays major roles in dependencies, compromise, acquiring—or more, cooperation with anger/angst, some design of infidelity, or embracing logic, ethics, the approval of peers, and the enhancement of various other legal or social boundaries. It is only in "church guise," together with the cinema, television, the nearly all of literature, and acceptable work, that allows or plays the predominant roles in allowing us the appearance of a normalcy, a self-acceptance, "en mass": "the charade" or the street, "everyday life," the participants' stability.

English folklore has given a wealth of fabled characters, some much loved and revered; King Arthur and his Round Table of knights is one such. He probably was a true identity, a good leader before the island began to be settled by other peoples. His courage and good character may, to some, represent a Christ figure with the disciples, but however that may be, he set as a mission for himself and his knights (ambassadors) to champion right in its perfection: thus, the "grail" construct championed by a worthy character. It is a very understandable venture, an understanding that somewhere in the now developed self that devotion can be stronger than in an unfulfilling circumstance, examples of which we have much written inside this arena, more than can be offered through a synopsis or formal thesis to expository completeness. One only has to note the history of martyrdom: as early as 978—King Edward, the first child martyr, the "boy king" at age fourteen, was stabbed to death by his stepmother who wished her own child to be king; the most recent martyr, he of modern times, Dietrich Bonoehoffer, a German Lutheran priest, was hanged by the Natzi regime because he held firm to his beliefs.

"Oneness," then, in the beginning supported physical survival, but the disclosure for that behavior was minimal, although there soon grew the need for some merit, some worthiness in communication with another; as our capacity evolved to include needs other than survival, the wished major ingredient of companionship became a paramount need. It could not come by force, quickness, or any physical quality; the increasing needs of the developing self/soul had grown to dimensions almost too great to fill, for they are not of physical mass but thought. The only method of continued psychological growth is through communication that enlightened and strong in wisdom, between one and another.

And so we come to man's deepest need—that for expression of self to another, so that acceptance is effected. The evaluation of this phenomenon is difficult to objectively commit to words for it is seated in the most unknown (unaware) abstract spaces of ourselves, these portions beginning to develop at/during the trauma of birth, only to be faced inevitably with death (at every turn) and finally—its dichotomy, paradoxical inconsistencies, ambivalence, irony, juxtapositions, opposites and untruths, beside the opening of genetic predispositions and their wares—and in these and more, we are given choices: choices of what or how much we wish to "do," and not wish to be known in our understanding of that we truthfully perceive of any one circumstance. And we must choose what portion of the "charade" we will embrace and what remains genuinely ours.

Too much emphasis cannot be attached to the principle of reciprocal giving, in the circumstance of oneness. It is almost a state of possession, which becomes a "one"—the single entity of a giving same. There is no dominance or subordination, however, exchanges perhaps, but no observable, no tangible inequities, cleavage—that loss of losses, should it occur, is drawn in by the lines of its absence—to not be but again restored.

As poetry uses repetition for presenting beauty, and truth, disclosure can be held up for scrutiny, again, in understanding the great need of oneness we all can experience.

Communication at a genuine level, now must occur, with trust being established. Disclosure can make clarity spring from a discussion, especially if there is a receiving party to the feelings needing expression. This oneness is found in reflection, at later hours, or in the anticipation in the present coming true. There emerges camaraderie, sensual stimulation, trust of most inner holdings, and a union of life philosophies, goals—being—all equaling the passion of some degree of full "companionate" love, if not completely: the freedom to experience one in a divine love relationship. Trust is perhaps the most frightening, if enduring, aspect of disclosure.

Oneness includes all negatives and positives, including some specific necessities: proximity, gender, certain personality traits, sentiment, camaraderie, libidinal resources. Yet, social class, education, interests—the list of needs is lengthy for it comprises in its separate pieces the whole, and they must, at the turn, lead to a functional degree, that which supports each party strongly.

The "lovely" of oneness is excitement, excitement interlocked or woven into the happiness of the partner, and as stated, a stance close to "possession" is in place, not in separate portions, but in reciprocal interactions of reality, equaling a kind of "one," a "oneness" close to religious faith or spiritual arrangement, and all of its attending properties, such as is expressed in the exquisite remark of the Little Prince concerning his true love, the flower:

My rose qui est unique au monde.

"My rose who is unique in all the world."
The Little Prince
the allegorical work, Antoine de Saint-Exúpery

There exist many steps in attaining the grail of oneness, and many are content, or unaware that there is not a full, a complete relationship. Many others, although they remain in a relationship, search, with pain and joy, always. Most individuals prefer to have a partner, not to live alone, males especially, and repeated efforts are made toward resolution. Much depends on the effort and sentiment that has already been shared in the current relationship, the necessary factor, as stated, being the existence of accumulative trust. Obviously, there can exist many levels of oneness in a relationship and scores of individuals have lived and died together—not at all with the fullness possible, but "enough." This circumstance is shown poignantly in the film *American Beauty* in which the protagonist in sweet reverie sees his marriage as full and good, a marriage in reality mundane, completely poor bourgeoise. This perception is caught at the moment of his impending death.

Truthfully, finding oneness is dangerous, allowing various avenues of abuse to be possible, both psychologically and physically. It is threatening for a relationship because of its strength in staying or leaving being dependent on what has already been invested, and so hurt is inevitable—

deceit, subordination—abuses of innumerable manifestations being possible, but the human animal is resilient, and usually only a residual remorse is left.

The progression of the growth of selfhood from dependency is toward more self- individuation. We want and need a oneness, communication, understanding, but we fear sharing this need with another, that we become vulnerable. We have come, then, to a curious juncture in our efforts to live as social animals: dependency, or some semblance thereof (all secrets, needs, ideas—deferring always to other— kept) or self-individuation with a free, open self, but alone, not with others on which to depend; we spend our days in vacillation of these two poles of "personhood."

Still the complexion of civilization is more the rose of oneness, although there is confusion of methods in achieving it. Older patterns remain, but in the confusion there appear new vistas.

All said, ought is but to look at an alternative to selfhood or individuation. There are many who seek this goal after its fashion. Technology has made possible numerous acquaintances, friendships, romantic involvements, work; there is much interaction between individuals, or perhaps demonstrable feelings, across great numbers of miles. Long distance affairs, marriages, and work do flourish in modern cultures. It might be informative, however, to study the degree of true oneness in these relationships—at this time.

Healthy individuation facilitates all other healthy relationships, and it should be one of our freedoms that is understood, if not in a worded document; it is one of our rights as social animals who live in groups. We are gregarious by nature and require understanding to, in some fashion, as circumstance permits, be given so by some others (acceptance). With this model there is usually a limited number of friends, associates, and colleagues if many of one's very own opinions, ideas, and thoughts.

Since cognitively we perceive ourselves as we feel others perceive us, all transmuted into a psychological self, which is in "love and charity," all particulars, properties, boundaries of our lives, it would appear necessary that the "self"—"oneness" dilemma, in order to avoid illness and unhappiness, we put aside the wisdom of "what price glory."

John Donne, the sixteenth-century British poet and priest, wished desperately for a oneness; he searched fervently through his faith, was long married with many children, but he could not find, to experience in satisfaction, his need fulfilled, the oneness he wished. His verses, their passion and beauty, beg his wish. His fervor, his wishes are best expressed in his lovely work "The Holy Sonnets," especially in Sonnet 14, "Batter my heart":

> take me to you, imprison me,
> for I except You
> enthrall me,
> never shall be free,
> never ever chaste,
> except you ravish me.

It might be that better steps would have been as the less demanding mortal seeker, to find in his seeking (the process) that which he sought in the must finding, objectively.

Self-disclosure, "telling our most known self to another," provides the steps, the long "bread crumb" path to the grail of oneness and choice called inside the charade of which we must choose. Extremes are not most often answers but are points of instruction. We cannot exist long or adjust to a fixed, extreme pattern. We must, then, work at modification and give all truthful effort to reaching a balance of self that compliments and embellishes others in relationships. Such is difficult and not our own, alone, recognizable accomplishment.

Happiness is a true fable: it is ephemeral in its everness. And we must live with this paradox to accomplish a balance. It cannot be done in demonstrable word or behavior, but only with self-knowledge and acceptance. It continues, still, and is the most difficult area of effort in our lives since all other manifestations spring from it. This sentiment was the major theme of the late nineteenth-century author Somerset Maugham, who wrote repeatedly using the theme of hypocrisy in Victorian society—"the way of all flesh"; these words state his most often theme of individuals' inability or failure to control their emotions.

These remarks prelude many of my kept awarenesses, as they have now in their present expressions, occurred. Some secrets rest in all of my work, but these come primarily from the verses written between the years 2000 and 2007; some few were written before those years, and after, and are found in different settings in this piece. The whole of the work is a continuous metaphorical free verse, divided as to subject and purpose of its creation. The work is, in its entirety, a true confessional, leaning toward a negative view of disclosure as the whole being is subject to greater loss, alongside its absolute necessity in our relationships. Since we do most often think in absolutes, the paradox is difficult, pushing us toward compromise and balance; as Robert Browning's, hero Andrea del Sarto, comments so, in a poor circumstance: "their strikes a balance." Life can be a feast, if not a fantasia of only lighted beauty.

Such is, now, here penned, a cathartic exercise in intuitive, perceptive understanding with a purposed hope that readers can more easily approach the stance of "Und die Spitzer" ("on the point")—to live truthfully and fully when the occasion demands, a sentiment well said, unknowingly, in answer to trivial questions by many others: "My life is my message," voiced in his own noblesse, Mahatma Gandhi.

Related Afterthought

In healthy ruminations concerning oneness with another, several avenues of thought bear our attention although it is almost a truism that we must seek oneness. Each one's other, with his positive and negative qualities, helps in understanding the beauty, but also the threat of oneness, or more repeatedly, achieving to its attainment. A word which has become very much heard in recent years in these such conversations, and not as a problematic property of adjustment, but a possible option in "singlehood." Many young people begin structuring their lives, their activities, and philosophies with this pattern of behavior as their carefully scrutinized and chosen pattern for living. Such is not to be confused with the popular criticism of our culture today: the preponderance of "meism"— not so—these individuals are usually psychologically and socially able, intelligent, and well-schooled with an interest in all areas of health. They care for others and are warm and passionate, the ascetic, for example, and unsuggestible; many of these individuals are celibate, some are, at times, promiscuous, and others choose alternative orientations. Their field of work is often demanding, but giving. They are not misanthropes or avoidant personalities. They simply enjoy enough sustenance, for whatever reason, within themselves, alone, to find fulfillment. They are productive, happy, creative, and fulfilled—with the vinegar and thorn of all experiences.

Such seems less to many, but we are stronger if we know ourselves well enough and can accept to enjoy "the plenty" to find a oneness in our own selves without major problems. This answer to adjustment is much more rare than oneness with another but is becoming more acceptable by the larger community. Individuals can find stability as well as those who must abnormally be happy only with other (Thenso).

The rebirth of thought, which began during the Renaissance, and is still present today, has seen the slowly, into quickly, now social, political, spiritual, and all other contributing areas advance the movement toward the acceptance of the self. Such does not must to imply "selfishness" but full selflessness, if the formula works into correctness.

Choosing someone or choosing to remain alone is not the only ingredient in this concern of oneness, but perhaps the most important. As in all major decisions in life, it is intensely personal.

Singlehood may be a type of metamorphosing adjustment, one of the products of the progress of mankind; we, more and more, separate ourselves from each other in ideology, physical activity, communication. Could that be such the way of remaining "the fittest"— surviving? Perhaps Arthur Miller, the early twentieth-century playwright, insightfully stated a truism in his play *Death of a Salesman*: "Life is a casting off." But the need is yet, present, and we are exacting from within for a oneness, which we truly seek in another; at times, there simply are questions—when at table or not—and the feast has no readily apparent answers or rather no simple, easily satisfying ones. It may be that we again defer, to time, and hear the words of Seneca: "It takes the whole of life to learn how to live."

PORTIONS

The world that waits for me at the top of the stairs
is one of supreme quiet, and invitation—
To a pensive time of varying mood,
strange and fanciful thought,
and ideas that burst like bright
exciting colors, over the furniture and appointments,
these alongside shadows, deep and grey—
This is the world of my most real self,
one of which I yearn, in paradoxical stances:
To escape, and to return—
for knowing one's self must be done in portions,
else the whole of it would crumble,
in the terrible and marvelous scrutiny,
as a castle,
fashioned,
of humble sand.
To be intimate with one's self is a brave and worthy task,
superseding that with any other.

INTRODUCTION

Beginning self-scrutiny, our point of departure (when Agatha's chest became closed), the fathers of the study of psychology had the area of philosophy, and beginning physiology, but only the first "scientific method" of the study of behavior. No hypothesis, theories, or laws were in place—only "naturalistic observation." Spontaneous behavior of the animal in its own environment, observed and recorded, was considered. Agatha's association with the arriving, more current theories came later with instruction and experience. Therefore, the assumptions and remarks appearing in this work are not scientifically founded, nor based on any one standing theory of human behavior.

For Agatha, the first wisdom of life is humility, long and long, and difficult. From the time of her early withdrawal and closure, statements are based on observation and experience, instruction and intuition married to personal perception inside illness—and the matter was a difficult one. Attempts were/have been made to, with emerging wisdoms, "fit" into the world which has been, and is, the current milieu; since "the world" has not always perceived similarly, and history is not closely that of another; closeted secrets have collected, always, yielding an approaching to feeling pressed with lack of expression of these—more the need for exclamation—of the difficult and the sweetness of ease. If one can be relieved—exorcised—of such a burden, such given over to someone worthy, he will more often find that he is closer to freedom as an individual. We feel that we are free, we want to be free, but in learning humility in conjunction with reason, our senses and other particulars, the "different" aspect comes to the fore; all are not free, as J. F. Kennedy remarked at the Berlin Wall: "As long as one is enslaved, all are not free" (whatever the barrier).

Writing then to release, to divulge, to praise, to express understanding and knowing—my knowing—to others has been the impetus to this narrative; with the drape removed, others may see increased opportunity for a more whole and fulfilled self. With this explanation, one might consider the work, in its complete, a confessional, to acuity in perception. Confession rests in disclosure. It can make clarity spring from exchanges, especially if there is a receiving party to the sentiments needing expression. This "oneness" is found in reflection or in the anticipation of the present coming true. There emerges camaraderie, sensual stimulation, truest of most inner holdings, and a union of life philosophies; goals being in all equaling, the passion of some degree of "companionate" love emerges, if not completely: the freedom to experience one in a divine love relationship. Trust is perhaps the most frightening if, enduring, aspect of disclosure.

The verses behind, then, are examples of disclosure of oneself, trusting to others' understanding; and camaraderie out of observation, instruction, and experience with the intuitiveness and insights through therapy. Such is formed and dressed metaphorically in free verse, with the strength of the silently mentored work of early American imagist poet, Emily Dickinson:

> if I win—
> if I lose,
> I will have had
> the transport of the aim.

AGATHA, MOI

Of a moment, I imagined that I have spoken,
about many things to others,
and when they stand by and look into my face,
I ask if I have spoken ought that I should not,
yet, in innocence's knowings, unacceptably.
And then, in my fancy, they respond,
"Oh no…it is only that we have not often
listened to the saying of so much right and good."
And then I sigh, with a pleased relief,
that I have loosed what I could not contain,
and I have pleased…I have found the center,
I have heard the true melody…and stars dress my
person.
I have spoken true…and I have pleased…and stars
dress me.
I will not reach for the sun and moon.

Elizabeth
From the work Chanson de Harold, 2011

THE *ECCLESIA*, OPENED

Lines, Sayings, and Parables

"Lines" are most often one, brief statement, offering a singular, found truth, particular to the author.

"Sayings" are often more brief, casual and rather not so didactical as proverbs; their insight is usually more personal if also applicable to many others, but do not so much approach the universal.

Simplicity is one aspect of the beauty of "sayings," if also a defect, but greater numbers benefit from these truths, not finding necessary experience, instruction, and other qualities which weave confusion into clarity and the finding of the fuller wisdom of the proverbs.

In objective reality, sayings tell us how to live together well and comfortably, which involves mediating sources of dissonance and strife. Proverbs teach us to live together beautifully, and well, with as little strife as possible and it, strife, dealt with through thoughtful, if moderated examples, reasoning behaviors rather than those with corporal or physical repercussions. Ideas and abstractions are more often together to produce truths.

As to style, "sayings" speak in the vernacular, while proverbs speak truth in royal verse. Both explain, instruct, advise, and admonish as true—justice. These can be found and award the peace of the humble whatever his station.

SAYINGS

Day, oh day, come, come quickly and stay at least into
an eon or so. Let the night be put
into a chest and the lock sealed,
for my soul cannot bear, more, these
darkness, the day dying over and again:
a pomegranate's cheek skeleton, a berry left,
seeking, the limb,
hanging as beaten wash,
that left after standing against the wind.

***

Speak love to me, although I
know our troth is
silent;
touch me with words that will practice
other fuller touch, and in a
spontaneous somehow,
I will know all love of thee.

***

—a happy pastoral idyll played out, and
the pen drawing its particulars—
it is then that beauty finds
beauty, and they together divide into
beauty, more,
heavenly spheres giving back again
to that whom innocence is, and
has been, groomed, and ebbing
and flowing,
the sweetness of gathered bliss.

***

When I am close to the riddle, it is even partially
unraveling; I am in, yet, a desert, where,
as charred fruit, all has been, and
all is, then, dry dust, dark cinder jewels—
except my insisting unseen—
but to my soul which has found, metaphorically,
release—
etchings, left in my imagined, but in
sentiment,
truthful drama, of individual pathos, not
at all, in humanity's scene, alone,
but mine alone:
ought but sweet memory, brought down
on the rains of time, left, and, alone.
Saddened, confused in reporting my most real feelings;
—this a time of uselessness and great void,
but truly alone.

***

Lavender's pungent, jeweled-alive marrow
and rose petals, with very violets;
centers, all,
touched by chamomile
gathered and dried, to be gently
bruised—
small entities of sweet fragrance
out the beauty of yesterday,
not lost, but brought into this
moment—
quiet time, god-time when my heart is open,
unafraid and giving to
new day.

***

Oh flower of knowing, open yet wide to me,
letting the center hold more than dreams
and promises have said, more
than the whole of the wisdom in the eyes
of (all) Abrahams.

***

Perhaps candlelight hides the untrue, and wet and
chill sharpen our thought to the good; perhaps
this stick has a presence from long,
former wanderings, finally out of itself.

***

darkened, haloed sweetness,
dutiful quiet, alone,
redeeming light, touched of shadow:
these questioning peace—
sweetness, pronounced of bitter,
solitude, empty to fair thought,
blooms of senses filling up with the forgotten, now
awakened—

***

Anniversary and great thanksgivings for
life and health, for the plan of a
knowing master,
a force, grande, such that there is no
touch possible, but only my
reaching into its constant finding.

***

I am intrigued by the child's mind,
its freshness, its malleability.
But I am fulfilled by the adult mind which,
by necessity, is filled with a
weariness, yet into wisdom, quite beyond
innocence.

***

I dreamed I dined on horse eggs and saw a
childhood autumn collage of pears
in their gold, persimmons,
"possum grapes," wild plums, golden rod,
and a treescape in a palette of brilliant
color.

***

Twilight inside closeted sunshine,
rain hanging in ambivalence—
But I can, yet, rise, and in so doing,
in my place, my fiefdom,
know my own noblesse.

***

Death ennobles all in its passing through,
whether with thoughtful good or
struggling error. We are spirit born
to, in death, unite in purity.

***

—but the moon, come, late, and fireflies
brought their light, their small torches,
in early summer's ritual dance,
awakening, that saved within, a perpetual feast—

***

I do not wish echoes brought of the holy man,
Job, for his trial is done,
and of him I know only example,
and my multitudinous woes, which in reality, was his all,
my recurring lamentations are not,
as a narrative, done.
But leave me this day, this peace, and in new dark
I will rise, ever, presently, to light, out will, gifted
of its mysterious, but constant and wise benefactor.

***

I have left this season, a dozen and
several more, of my father's Cape Jasmine
blossoms, not to grace my
rooms, but to waste their all beauty
on my outside rooms—
so much the world has been with me,
my heart divided, yet, confused
in its wantings, and
following, its musings.

***

All I am is all I have

***

—The eternal saga of passion and resting,
the potent moment rising
in its newness, a toned virelay—

***

When our thoughts struggle,
and our hands grasp,
when we weep in glorious harmony,
we stand taller than we are,
becoming the very fancy we embrace.

***

New brought bread,
left on the cabinet to grow, in its
wait, mold from its fresh, moist
self;
for it is wet, virile, alive, if briefly
and is not, in any way, complimented
by the refrigerator, except to become an image only
of existing: how so like men in
their varietal decisions to be.

***

—My place, my gentle pied-à-terre, a gallery
of thought and feeling, will thrashing
about, circumstance and resulting
sentiments.

***

As the bird flies into tomorrow,
as leaves quiver in soft
winds,
as morning is born in
simple, seasonal waves
of quietly coming light—
could not but love of good passion
lie gently about me.

***

summer's early evening, too warm, but only speaking
the season;
remembering that I have forgotten all of the summer
evenings of several decades, those filed
away bathed in gin and quarreling,
sinking despair—

***

I thought of you often, over, quickly, wishfully often,
for it is our fancies that lie our true realities, those
our hearts know though our arms do not embrace,
and our steps not to wing towardward, our eyes open
onto.

***

O my soul, self
of a beggar soul,
remind often that there is Presence
everywhere, and as the petals,
of a flower arrange in patterns,
there also are those outside
and to the inside of the fuller pattern.

***

Parables/Riddles

the complete, rich indulgence in innocent contemplation,
and decided joy in entering, bequeaths
the heart perpetual peace,
and holds, in silence, a volatile finality.

***

Every moment, a drop of purest gold,
the dancing light of the perfect,
angelic-faced diamond,
the thousands of sapphire pointes
in a glance to the sky's faery blue—
every moment, already given, give me again
in taking—out this first gift,
of life.

***

but by the eternal directive of
seasonal order, brought into
absence, it rising into
another, infinite
second being,
the first, its summer,
its generous, radiant
summer,
lost.
And so, September mornings
become, more, the
bittersweet.

***

under Medieval light in my sitting room,
music, fatigue, alone,
the acquiescing a seemingly forward step—

***

yet my heart is long and long, through yesterday
into tomorrow, with a sweetness that
nourishes beginnings and their
conclusions.

**

—moon, that another summer's
rain will fall onto empty
summer record, and those joys of it,
which are,
will flow into another September,
not quite finding her purist sweet
olive, and I will be cold again,
and I will be, in the
all of it, most pure in my
alone.

**

A truly lonely woman is one who,
by her social custom, must,
puts out her garbage,
in winter's cold, even during
holiday.

**

of my space, hanging between the hounds,
almost to touching and tearing, to
be thrown into the river,
and yet, still, I do not fall, potions,
surely disguised hounds,
holding me to this side.

**

In the moment, beauty is arrived, its flaws
woven out, into a select piece, hopefully
with an elixir of pain enough
to assure the catching of all the
next arriving, all of newly fair.

***

Near and far, the day in hand
can have been a magnificent share
of raw wealth
of which our lives can say in
one splendid, passing moment.

***

Light in the heart, a gift, grooms a
shield to fend, of life, all its
dragons.

***

To be impatient is to, sometimes, overlook a small,
exquisite gem, expecting a larger, that is also conditional.

***

And I wept, for blessed is the heart
that can feel, but cursed almost more, is
the heart that feels alone.

***

The fingers of cool smooth my skin,
the silence of attack reaches out;
come, come morning time and
let me warm in forward steps,
maneuvers of thought and the silent holding of
lovely flesh.

***

Could winding smoke, upward,
chilled rose lying all across;
could wheels turning; voices closing silence
could these, indeed, be truth, now.

**

I am in the darkened way, and blest I
am found, for I hear autumn rain,
and within it helping, keeping voices,
hope joyful, such as
the lamp lighted.

**

Rose, the color my mother gave to me,
in her dark sun, her quiet
passion,
in pain and trepidation yielding
a mirror of reflected gold to my spirit.

**

The hermit, the hero, the saint are our expressions
and drawings, and when we cannot,
the circle, in its fullness,
is drawn into the argument, the string
tied at either end.
I yet fear, but I, yet, hope.

**

Every man, no matter his fashioning, stance, or
sentiments, is made more good, more holy
in his passing through death, for
he, willingly or not, succumbs to natural
law which is portion of the
all good.

**

And we know
that whatever the heart speaks to reason,
so that memory is born,
does not fear the struggle to be,
only to know that it can never,
as yesteryear snows gathered,
or the cliff's check erased of moving angel wings;
—joining these,
it can never recall
the full beauty of beauty passed:
a summer day,
finding the flower into berry,
the leaf within sunlight,
and with its comparison,
ascribing compliment utmost and sovereign,
chosen from every store,
a sonnet once to hold complete love and loveliness.

***

HolyfatherGod, leave to me this closing
evening the reality of the
permanence, the resilience,
the enduring, the completely
loving power of the soul,
the "again," when all has been,
the impossible turn, given, felt, and known.
Cotton stalks, brown tissue-like, broken
in being turned under; seed sent out into its
season, sorrow, joy—oh the breadth and depth,
the heart spread wide, the soul,
that we continue.

***

the flower must wait her season
to sing her verse—and
to these all lie the
sentiment
of happiness,
each being found as peace
in a holy place,
happiness each, for of itself,
in the patience it extends
to wisdom out love
in its
reaching and in
its steps.

***

Being put aside is like being in the
wilderness, the limberlost,
even away from oneself, having left one's
heart with those banishing, suddenly
more dear, in the casting off—
for when something, someone—falls away,
there is a small weeping, at least,
for the good in the lost
part.

***

As my lashes opened and closed, quickly, in the
pulsating brightness of the splendid round
of light, I saw haloes, rainbows
complete, every color that could grace a
full palette—awe and honor to
the natural, the very face of spirit being.
I want to be in it and let it bathe me beautiful;
and in the beauty know content,
catching, in part, my impatient
bliss.

***

But renaissance had shadowed these hours, and like
a vessel, full round and filled to opening,
newness waited its moment,
its birthing sounds already heard.
The answering grey, a wet, cold drape,
will fall to reveal a season that is
recorded, always, known
to the child who sees out from within
our fuller selves.

***

Everything has been before, record of its
being and passing in our thought,
and to its newness and beauty
we give out our larder held and open
to these such visitations, sweet
review within natural widening, and
the emancipation of saved
seed, and its promise, into a moment's
flower.

***

the seed into its womb of its fertile
chamber, to emerge, all,
into the glory of idea awake, the idea aware,
I, ilet, my soul passing
through its windows,
beauty made more beauty
in faithful exchange.

***

Tragedy courts polarization in thought and in
winds of such defeat; we look back to
ripe cherries, golden pears, hanging
tender snow on chilled evergreen and pine,
that bending that which might have could.

***

Eldest vessel of thy father's seed,
baring statue and visage, I bring in saddened
reverie, flowers and place at your feet,
this time of season, occasioned of unhappiest
circumstance.

***

I offer the content of the stick or the hand:
the stick is the flower of the two,
for it embellishes, in the strength
of winds, those of thought and those
of celestial spaces;
it holds throughout claspings, not
to pull away in mood or
circumstance.
It blooms out a sameness throughout
all seasons, and a ring or bejeweled
arrangement neither enhances
nor diminishes.
In truest wisdom, then, I offer the stick
as companion,
the hand as sport.

***

I became who I am in the ongoing epic
of awareness, realization and acceptance,
in the all;
and I became the handsome peacock,
spreading its fan or color
inside,
and not a moment in place or time,
but in steps helped along by shadowed
spirits who hold me up so that
I walk through these
steps, as they become still others more.
I, coming to know toward
peace,
salvation without properties, but
sentiment, alone, to accompany
me.

***

Heavy is our journey, casting off old skins
when they can no longer cover
our metamorphosing interior selves,
very pathos of we who think and feel
is knowing the bright beauty of scales
and feathers passed.

***

Against the dimming of those that follow
matroned summers, to remain in,
while stepping away, from the
innocent familiar to the resignation
of the greatest unfamiliar, engenders
sainthood to all who hear the tenor's flower
and dogs barking in first summer,
to know in them and yet to
press with honesty beside
resignation, peace in the backward face of
remembrance, and in the bramble of the
truest adventure, the forward.

***

Warm friendship, and deep night
conversation, souls finding
confession,
and, in it, strength, out of coals
covered and kept
for such this hour, this revealing
flourishing, light to matters having lain
dark, rising then even as truth,
a magnificent violent flame.

***

I am, in my whole, a sleep of sorrowful
dark, its constancy arising out of
potions,
heavy and true, of awareness
and knowings.

***

My heart has been absent its words,
not requiring the blood of
my pen,
the grave Spartan of Lenten thought.

***

flowering into the beauty of
passions and truth, to distance
and smile with an ivory glance in
her matroned autumn:
so beautiful, spring, garden of hope
and purist joy, etched about
by the bittersweetness of its
brevity and even elusive
capture.

***

Night: that grande plateau in time
when loneliness finds a
sanctuary, and the heart hosts,
aching, its guest—

***

Scarlet impatience, giving over to the
hours of their capture,
resplendent in their giving,
beauty used up into an
abundance—

***

Gardenia in August: summerlude widening
past the firefly and a menagerie of
yellow butterflies, into autumn's warm
glow, her melancholy smile—
an omen, a pronouncement—
a reprieve;
surely the elixir of time has effected
the gift of golden mead to
flow within cool dews.
—On discovering an August bloom on a
"second generation" gardenia,
after seeking its whiteness for several
days, thinking it to be sunlight glistening
on new growth—bringing
to my thought these images, above—

***

Capture can be accomplished with color and form, the illusion
of movement, these holding more to heighten sentiment, to
arrange memory—a glance toward, a glance away, and back
again to new day; this primordial ritual—felt and imprinted:
but only in the experience of the unfolding do we stand truly awed
and condemned.

***

Each moment of silence that falls away
sounds as words of lamenting
verse,
the dark melody of the dirge,
the petal's gentle struggle to depart
its centras;
yet, the kaleidoscope of yesterday within
the turnings of thought,
these against the very despair of soon approaching,
beautiful eventide, inside its
beautiful evensong—the words:
farewell, farewell, farewell.

***

The very heaviness, the bittersweet
musings,
the abject pain in fullest
crying out, our hearts
touting our unknowing, and the
poor secrets
that we will find in
writ and doctrine—
playthings, toys—rope and
marbles,
when the full shadow
is come.

***

I must bear, as conclusion wills
to me, with the pain in silence
of the absent wall clock,
as the stretching binding of the
rapidly ascending of the
ponderous bamboo,
as the emptiness brought on the
photograph,
in the stuffing down with prayers
and promises,
the heart almost to give over
to something that would
offer a sweet oblivion;
—but the struggling down will work
straight the back, a
squaring of shoulders, a chocolate
in hand—
these to finish the steps of day,
and enter those of the
night.

**

into, into flows still a river,
flaming gold, light, within
the day,
flaming gold, deep within
the day.

**

Pretender to truth, the wisdom is more harsh, and abiding,
than night mists or daytime sounds,
yet petals losing capture;
we clothe it in guises pleasing, but in the
hollow of our most sensitive self,
we know that what is, must come not
to be, often sometimes in a slow
fading, or perhaps, quickly, with decisiveness,
all of it put quite aside, and reflection then
no more than a lamp quieted of its bloom.
In these moments, mine is more a slow fading,
in a garden pregnant with a heavy
draught of forgetfulness that
comes to leave a bramble of emptiness,
a flame leaping to its dying,
a small passing of soul which approaches
the poignancy of the matter of a
brief knowing of our being.

***

Cares and realizations, acknowledging and
Accepting—all feather and wool me
in company of truth and
good.

***

Dream faces, the bells too intense:
sunlight greater than its metaphorical
descriptions;
thought that haunts as sensuous expectancy:
Ah, time, bide me; I am filled
with thy gifts!

***

Waiting is a holy instruction; this
understanding, an entrance—

***

How poignantly the music speaks—
of now, then, ever—

***

For I came to know at twilight the sting of truth, if
softened by beauty; but it is the grail I have ever
sought, trying, struggling with finding ultimate
beauty in its wisdom, the dark, the hurting, the
emptiness beside an always, sometimes, fullness,
wrapped in the infant's trust and peace.

***

Hell in its sweet, heaven in its bitter.

***

Oh babe, oh Elizabeth, I donning
royalty, and we all—
we cannot marry our spirits
for we are one alone, except, perhaps,
within a moment of innocent
pastoral memory, a berceuse, almost
suggesting, petals whose flesh
always surprise in decay.
Let us gather moments.

***

LINES

—the hidden, stolen hours of night:
the birthing—grasping, frantically—
the hours of early morning—

***

Blackberry blossoms, politely arranging
within the morning's sunlight,
dancing among thistle and briar,
on roadsides, still, their promise, a happy
wager to the children who sleep in my heart,
awakened yet another Easter,
pastels and new warmth embracing my
waiting need,
wrapping it in arms that can reach only
from yesterday.

***

Within these scapes, the sweet brings
longing, and the beautiful a
mourning,
these caught up in the whispered
smoke of knowing—that of
tainting, apology, and conclusion.

***

I should be happy this early morning,
and I am, in part, but
I know the race
is ever, and I anticipate, truly
feel now, ladened,
precious, the
gold of fatigue,
the potion, the unseen,
relentless absolution that
fires all my days;

***

—always, before and after
the falls, the descents,
the deaths that give birth
to the cursed cycles,
the yoyo, the dark.

***

Grieving lost affections, busy with strategies
for wholeness, praying for direction,
these conscience requiring;
nien—all that will heal:
simplicity within the complex is the
requirement of untampered and truly
not at all ostentatious truth, and
complexities will flow but with the tide.

***

whatever the truth, whatever the plan, in whosoever
hands matters will come to find,
my petition begs their togetherness,
in peace complete, knowing joy, and rest
from their work, their incredibly
difficult sojourn.

***

My heart has been absent its song,
images forgetting the dark issue of my
lonely, yet into my thought—
for I have heard no laughter in these
days now, and bright yellow
daisies offer their gold in apology
to the rarer gold that sounds
in yesterday.

***

The singular principal in the narrative, in the orders
of his priestly comforting, stated: It is one of the great
miseries of mankind that we do forget.
Andso, I sat in place, at peace with my companion
postulate—all is as I wish—for that is all
there is.
Ah, redemption—but the vinegar and the thorns—

***

Dove and lily, weep for me,
the rainfall of my heart's own colors.
All that is before—

***

and then I was calm; somehow a decision was made;
so strange—the unreason in malady, and I began to
climb out the spiraling despair, and today is beauty
embraced and held, beyond description, a bliss joyous,
if inconstant—advance of progressive spiraling
downward, I reach for discipline, strength, and hope,
a construct I do not fully understand or hold complete
in its supposed essence.
Resignation spreads as a fan, and my pen is quieting my
stones, now, still sparkling in laughter and freedom, but like a
large, dark bird is spread out in the distance, its plumes
preparing to write the next time.

***

Gardenias, my lost gardenias, you are together
with me, each the treasure
of the thousand of you;
my thousand white gardenias,
trembling beneath, in your knowing,
of the new, into fullest passion,
of Rose and Chestnut, white fragrance
whose certain dying lay a writ
unpublished, left only to helplessly
unfold; and passion, whose
quieting remained a secret kept, breath
and touch finding its dark in their
unacknowledged, losing strength.

***

I am, in my whole, a sleep of sorrowful
dark, its constancy arising out of
potions,
heavy and true, of awareness
and understanding.

***

Suggested moonlight lay about upon all its
familiarity, darkness and shadow
finding a verse,
a partial line in deep night,
April 10, 2001,
the image reached for, forgotten.

***

Oh night, your unsung beauty speaks
to me in unsung metaphor,
which cannot live to be
caught into description.

**

to wandering into a watchful, indulgent half-sleep,
where yesterday flowed in and out,
her dance a beautiful song,
a familiar, southern lamenting; and joy
came, still, and found, within even
the chiding of the requiring, waking present,
unfolded, wrappings laid aside—
the lost, another glory left, waiting her season,
the wise, bruising to touch, and loss,
into a final satisfaction.

**

it all, in the span of a day or a season,
even yet our each gift is numbered, truth and fancy
fill, to satisfy our thought,
and time takes away the
raveling, leftover, clarifying
threads.
Of J., our long togetherness that was only an empty
hour stretched out, with colors that were, at times
an apparent true, but to quickly fade to barren other—

**

and together with the exquisite yellow
of duet honeysuckle, may this
blessing
fill thy soul with peace and truth,
the very gold of love,
both select and rare:
gathering toward thee now, my adagio
of hope.

***

Ah, Morpheous, visit me with a
long, sweet draught
which will take all but the pleasurable
ambiance
of lavender, resting, yet, of rainfall, gentle, still;
of the hour that flies, but leaving those ever young,
of the giving in love, of my heart, alone—
accepted, enough.

***

The heavy flowing, the very torrent of insistent
and impatiently eager, into the disquieting
bramble of my thought
passes over, quite without attention, to twilight's
stars touching waiting berries, those
hanging in their found heaviness,
unknown to any other than my memory's dark;
or in the put away, the faithful whippoorwill at
beginning eventide who is marked, into
exile, with its plaintive mourning—

***

As tears that cannot know their most loveliness
in spontaneous falling, this escape,
more and more, binds me, my capture
of a leftover feast, an abundant, spent
knowing of self, among, I and they,
a shadowed galley of souls lost to each
other in what we could, speaking
the quiet of unforgiving winds,
becoming repeated, continuing tempests, ever into
their past.

***

And memory touches from behind, expected,
almost wished for, the sweetest
movement of all: beauty,
love, and peace passed
through and left without any complexion
but rarest and pure.

***

There is no awakening, no consciousness,
no expectancy or promise—
not, yet, remembrance—as truly significant as the
coming in of day;
life has, surely, its bent of the crushing
chariot wheel, in its battle
regalia, entire, but also the image of the
beginning, again—of light—out the
full darkness just passed through.
And it is this image, and all of its
assemblage of thought, to which we mortals,
we "lesser gods," do hold.

***

When cool breadth rides in on the moving
paths of ribboned dark, candles
and shadows, the constant pendulum,
and sweet music of string and horn
companion well to the singular bell—well
and well, and as the hem sewed, carefully,
finishing and holding, containing the garment—
these small touches enlarge, becoming supportive
to the heart's composure,
down distant halls, deep and secret chambers,
and small jeweled caskets—these with their
dreams which never will.

***

—House of knowing, offer prayers and
oblations, that strength hold,
and every dewdrop be
lovingly gathered before it slips
into the meadow of the day.

***

I am leaves casting shadows of the season,
in sunlight, yet, still yet, in
moonlight;
my worded thought is, indeed, gold,
whose underside smiles out
worthy silver.
Let mystic fingers turn them about,
over and again.

***

our lamentations heard against the distant,
almost faltering, in still another
genesis, this, the glow of the rising;
and we, as so within, the new, old struggle,
only more, we, in the hand of nothing,
a beautiful, illusive nothing:
nada—
and with these such comfort only,
the day's morning laughter echoing
a continual farewelling,
we wander, in a fullness of fatigue,
into the eternal night of time past.

***

Coming to me were
Christmas rounds of handsome green,
empire into shadowed dark,
dressed with scarlet water,
brightness embracing
waiting, hued darkness,
somber and beautiful,
quietly speaking again
promised grace bestowed,
blood drops upon a tree.
Colored deep are the secrets
out of the vine of Jessie.

***

giving up laughter
in ditches whose sand became
the sensual innocent; and in the
softness of finishing rain, the
spent breathing of short
passion,
summer chariots echo, and their gold
is stored, far inside the heart's
well, to sound, in their silence,
in the long, deep river of gentlest
embered, imaged thought.

***

Coming full round the hour, I gratefully lay
my head upon my folded arm, for I have
already reached for the sweet nothingness
of my dolls.

***

Inside reason, we, inside our rooms, are safe
from a variety of winds, but our thought,
our consciousness no longer blind of
light, dull of noise, tender into clarity
of touch—our thought our
inside knowing blow strong and with
pernicious intent to lash our backs
and cause to bend.
And if we fall to bending, standing again
is not certain, certain not to be as before.

***

In the night no man can foretell what a day
will bring: a peacock or a broken stick,
these trailing opulent color and grace,
or thwarting the irregular, the curious obtuse,
the strangely ungood.

***

my thought out the recesses of my reason,
as I stood, at last, able, able
to voice it: there is nothing
save will and circumstance, will being
drawn when actions know consequences.

***

Haloes, crystal images of forgotten hours;
whispers, gold graciously left over,
and echoes, like moonsilver—these be the warmth
that fill up my
needing, reaching hands.

***

And, thenso, we find only the self
we can allow, and out of
fear of its whole, we
sacrifice that lovely and helping,
approaching with
seductive wiles toward peace,
but without blossom in
hand,
or learned sayings, pleasing;
without any on our part by need,
rather than our prize; we stumble,
and within, find even greater need.

***

and summer's splendid fulfilling, in a season
of death:
It is escaped in no part of my being, and, yet, I
know only enough to be perplexed. Beautiful words,
saddened expressions, courageous and
glorious goodbyes—all have come from the page, and
some from heard utterances.
But—the ever present, the ever was, the ever be—
still, even if the bramble be untwined
in the doing of it.
Oh, mountain, will there be a dream in the sleep.
And I wander with a weariness at the end glance,
the last word, the final step.

**

A cup, a candle, the light of lamps
on autumn's full glory;
the sounds of bells ringing in eternis—
angels drawing in the day.

**

I hear winter birdcalls today;
geese fly early through my south trees—
lonely sounds in cold spaces:
the heart joins in their movement,
and the joy of earlier radiance,
very light from Raphael's raiment,
become already, so soon, a half
dream, within the silence of ringing bells,
as many as grains of sand.

**

significance—only in the moment, close and elusive,
the energy broken free to combine with all
other, to pass familiarity and knowing,
to perhaps combine in new monarchs and
their masses, but ultimately to
be reduced to energy with identity, to
final resting—perhaps—the only answer
to the eternal riddle which holds our
moments and we the players.

***

...beautiful fancy against reality...
but no, there are winds, and night birds,
thoughts pushed back, pressing into
the fore,
nature's insisting—and bells, and calls,
voices and songs inside new,
first light—
the reprieve stands small to the punishing
constant,
so known by dramatic contrast.

***

Could light be ever,
glory of conscious thought, the
pathway surely to the place of God;
Oh, leaf of darkness,
turn, turn quickly, and often,
your mirror finding underside promise
of overside bliss.

***

I, yet, see and feel,
but the light is dying within so that
I see, most, and not with anticipation, what is to be,
and reflection, sweet, of that which has, to me,
already been.

***

I parade and speak on a stage where origin and props
are in distance too great to review—and oh God,
I will act, respond and die to cues misspoken,
mispronounced, carelessly offered.

***

The forces of evil do work, empowered, if only
inside one's thought. The threat is real, a reality
in prospective truth; and so the response is in like
kind.

***

The webs and twines, the brambled knots
of desire—of esteem, sensation,
immortality--
weave, as surely, together, as those of
corporal—abject—want and need.

***

There is, with very constancy, a falling away.

***

How sad, how inconsolable: my truest, most
passionate lover, the whole of the glorious
natural, as an Adonis, ever reappearing and farewelling.

***

In the path, steps are not numbered; they are felt.

***

Can it be that love is within itself, to be
without only by the song of another.

***

If death closes all, then it does so through an open door.

***

Brownskins under rainbows, maypops after dewberries;
blackbirds and leaf-stars, and wood fires and cold
skies: a treasure ephemeral—innocence; yesterday

***

Could it be that through love we find all the answers
and embrace the questions as little children.

***

A rose is fragranced reality; let me, please, walk one path through
this breathing, effervescent garden of become spirited flesh.

***

The air cools, the sky shadows, the behindward advances.

***

If I could reach to touch, how sweet the objected flesh,
its texture, its fragrance, its truest hue,
that of its purist truth and passion.
Ah, ecstasy in the terrestrial round.

***

We have our years, and then we catch our moments,
desperate reflection and expectation, these to fall to the
darkened fantasia of memory, death held back.

***

significance: billowing smoke
into the undistinguishable

***

the intractable rock of alone,
can alone, offer the bringing,
one giving together.

***

the lock must hold, the thread not break:
can the round come to close, please—
a candle, a fragrance
burning,
and hope, more in simple honesty
than the gnarled, obtuse
dalliance of fear with despair—
please, Thee, please Thee, the lock the thread,
only of Thee Abba, please.
Amen

***

Can hope flourish inside unhappy
realities—
let me lay my pen and glasses
aside for I have
drowned my muse with my sorrows,
my lamentations out days
now passed;
fear stifles spontaneity, and
soft thought,
and few wisdoms are found in full defeat.

***

Every separate hurting we feel
is a small forgiving
of our loss.

***

The quiet became a nectar I drank as queen upon
her splendid couch, its tasting full with
birdsongs wandering into distant
light, and memory.

***

I watch you through your voice, in your
larger struggle, but, too, in the
roll call of smaller pathos;
and I love you in a kind of
desperation, wishing that
I could gather the both of your soul
into arms of just a small,
comforting safety,
and that over and again.

***

Can they not come quickly, their potions,
sweet relief—how safe to feel they
are nearby, to forbid the real
and anoint oblivion: the turn is
sharp and true, however, paradoxically ironic,
as they, when their potions are spent,
give back the light and consciousness,
and more, great lamentations through memory, that
accompany the hours until they,
of necessity, must visit again.

***

How sweet these, how sweet consciousness
and thought, greater, before the
fatigue of hours:
greater than the iris in royal purple
nobly pleasing;
greater than the sun,
its splendid and altogether grande, flowing nectar—
greater than the innocent, greenest blade of
promise to forward and upward
leanings.

***

If the small seed can bring a uniquely lovely
blade, the wind bear the softly feminine, single
crepe myrtle floret into the wider openness—a
moment, a moment—the noble bamboo sing
perseverance in constancy—can we not remain
present, after some fashion, in our left absence.

***

With humbled silence and the bow of true belief—
reach forth as poetry, with the
strength, perhaps, of beauty, alone,
but devout and humble
prayers offered draw verse which
angels sing,
at divine request.

***

I fear the ashen cheek will become
the more familiar image of the
ties between us, for me
ashen near to death of a sweetness,
for thee, perhaps surprise or
merely inconstancy which offers
hope to hurt, and in a moment
obvious dismissal.

***

Ah, the tree's shadow, and that of the
wall, but it is the bird in flight
that takes our steps,
our thought,
into the placid sea.

***

—And so, it may be that all that is,
is a special arrangement of the
Divine, and each of our moments
a unique drama which unfolds
within it, with excitement and a measure of
grandeur.

***

How close leans the grey, cold reminding need
for touch, that that in Camelot not become memory
alone, but memory of the nightingale's
drawing of beauty into twilight,
yet beauty still.

***

Does fire always, in its trying,
always purify, but
rather, without justice
or mercy,
consume.
I am old and tired,
and my remaining, insistent fire
finds an impotent vessel in which to burn.

***

the malaise, spreading the peacock
of pathos—
and, always, the hunter, fancied,
given able to strike over and again
into my will:
why do I yet run, wounds
aside, only knowing.

***

And so we joust to convince that we win
in peace, to, with pain never to be drawn,
know that we are each, only each,
with companion merely inside or to the
fore of our shadow.

***

Grant us peace, not in repose,
but in the feast;
for all can gift death,
but only of Thee is life.
Indulge us with the bounty of Thy
Blessings,
we all, of every Israel, in the
steps of each Adam: and from Thy
table let us find peace of
slumber,
dreams bright in darkest night,
hope born of our lineage
out Holy Loins,
Celestial birthright.
Heavy angst of many demons—

***

Lamps are tired, yet continue to
bloom out into the room. Mozart's
piece haloing adds warm love
beginning and ending to my
thought—how ought
but to look behind and see how far
the journey is forgiven—
Oh, Mamma.

***

The monarch butterfly has its season,
and its port of flower; ah, butterfly
and me: I wonder that our
musings might be guests together
at the table of day. I have
seen the smile in butterflies, but I
have, not ever, heard their
laughter,
in any corner of my garden,
a circumstance the truest night
of separation.

***

In strangest climes of images, silent thought, I sometimes
enjoy waking early, to think, observe, feel
the good that can be, and yesterday
smiles to me; and there is present no regret,
no fear, no ponderance of small worlds
and their great questions.

***

My physical pain is only reflection of that of my heart,
with the very incisive thrust of memory.
I am nothing, I wish nothing other than the cessation of thought,
an absence of sentiment, and conclusion of memory—
and a paling to my wounded spirit, a respite to embrace.

***

My days are being pirated by the mundane needs of others, selfish need,
if unknown to these others. I am losing my touch with
self, my grooming of thought and idea.
—must act, defend, and conquer, with truth,
honor, and good.
In retrospect, such has ever been, but such does not
need ever be.

***

God is good, in every step,
purposed or in thoughts: those
with each shadow that moves,
with every sunray which enters, into;
the moments gather, His gifts,
to fill up every poverty, and the day
becomes a magnanimous treasure,
a basket, an urn, a cloth tied full,
with beauty and grace.

***

For I have much to lose, and
did not know until only this
moment's inventory; that
to gain is only of fancy, and
its worth, a coin without
marking,
And so the veil hangs over
today.

***

And so, stay the while with me, mirror
to the sting of my existential;
for the sting is carried within
these beauty, and, again, warm,
wet flesh in its very dress
of opulence enjoys, knowing all the
while that after the steel
glow, the golden eye, and all the
orchestration of their continuing ceremony:
it is the warming, the
holding, the pain of giving
up that beauty arranges in such
this sting as one of early autumn's
sunsets.

***

But O anchorite, take to your empty cell,
for, of love at all,
there is the must of
wounding.

***

I must petition before the whirlwind,
and know my strength as I stand,
my back envisioning
comrades in legions, their hands
supporting its panels of tired flesh;
But when his harshness was spoken,
I did not know of the coming
whirlwind,
and my hurt was certain, but
small, and not fearful;

and the nation of petition did
not come to me, not for a great time.
I repent me of waiting so long, and
forgetting, still, yet, to ask, what
confidence I can
gather,
gathering from the God of
self.

***

—the harpies! livered host, in pieces bloody and scabbed,
experiences no pain ought past knowing,
or contempt, slighting or purposeful rebuke—

***

And I knew the tumbleweed to be noble,
the posture ascribed to all having of death, all
wanderers made worthy,
not knowing the path, but, with steps
hesitant or eager, entering into the
truest moment of self,
to begin, complete, into fabled dark or light.

***

The tortuous quiet in solitude, yet ordained
of peace, with gentle fingers, labors
toward soothing wounds
and weariness of responding;
Still, in the tender since in their reaching,
rests no accompaniment of voice, or step,
yet smile or touch.
If could could be a garden in some distant
Corner, which houses a heart with
these cares, then I would
find my peace in quiet oneness, to be
alone in togetherness, to know
spirit bound into truest freedom.

***

Rapture pouring out passion kept,
as fire of purgatory promising;
issue forth, let me burn,
let me be pulled down by wet
and weakness in my moments
of sweetest sentiment;
If in words, or glance aside, or more
touch together, September is yet only a
season between, and married
together the joys of all climes,
allowing moments of golden
laughter whose throat is
still of fullest promised green.

***

If I could think my ideas all the way out, I
would not, in oftentimes now,
for the thoughts would not be true, or if they
should be, they would represent no reality.
In theory is the only purity, for as it plays out,
it becomes, invariably, partially,
if not wholly, unclear,
not knowingly true.

***

—So mercurial the sounds of the
lyre our hearts be.

***

—Oh for the peace that must, surely,
issue out love's constancy.

***

I cannot hold on to the content I sometimes
feel, even in the crystal of its moment.
It becomes transparent and I see through it
to all of my waiting, unhappy notions.

***

Today's winds blow, curiously, elegiac, drawing out
a scroll of yesterday, for we cannot
lose it because we stand, today,
already in it, beside voices and
smiles, touch and sighs:
early autumn, the beautiful pain of summer
lost, leaving September, always,
first to grieve.

***

—And words of pleasing verse sounded
in my thought, that cares rest
easily aside, against
recorded beauty of love.
These passing, but satin ribbons, tied together
in perfect French knots, with small nosegays (this beauty and love)
about, these will bring me into them again.
—a manner of keeping a balance—remembering beauty, peace
I have known—

***

Everything is nothing, and the nothing embraces the all.

***

Conjecture is the reality we grasp to walk, not wander the path, and in
its questioning lies the final, waiting peace

***

The condition closest to all of our awareness in our mortality;
to marry the two together, comfortably, we must love and hope,
and look, quickly, if impotently, away,
when even these cannot be comfort enough.

***

leaves, and my nourishment of them,
and enjoined to acceptance,
not in shadow of memory but in
pause
before the certain rondo begins again.

***

Mourning dove and roses are with me,
still, and speak their verse
to me.
September, September, the tears
inside your signs make
visitation in my heart beside
those over on the other side.
Sweet, sweet, my portion, even
as all of Israel, bittersweet,
autumn wild plum
in their all fragrance,
bittersweet.

***

—a feast becoming, and at table, but to fall
in tasting, even to fullness, from table to
desert, famine and night.
And there are those, found outside the feast, by design or what,
who never tasted, and they, too, fall.

***

Echoes of a ascending concerto;
these echoes allow a sweet capture
of my cries through angel hands,
placing these into a heavenly urn,
to someday be poured over
me,
that I be cleansed and prepared for
closing and silence,
my hunter no more looking before in
question, behind in fear.

***

Another closing—the circular phenomenon, quickly,
so much haste—now aware, seizes my timorous heart.

***

The wall clock strikes the bird away into
memory; a shadow, a light,
a candle waiting
within wayfaring violet and rose,
captured away from the better bramble,
into the now, of yesterday.

***

Can one not experience the moment,
after some fashion, without knowing
conclusion and yesterday, and
holding, impotent, will;
yet that tomorrow will reflect today.
This season's first whippoorwill is
repeating his song outside my
open door, inviting in the
soft darkness, just as in his season,
the year past—
and so,
we are only more steps into what
becomes mystery in its sameness;
Hope, love, peace—these find in loneliness
alone;
oh God, how weary I am:
seasons, the day, clocks—
flowers in their morning's wealth,
penniless at dusk.

***

as it came in my night just passed,
the images combined: HolyfatherGod, let me die,
of Thee, and not of me.

***

Secrets, in their boundless silence,
make great soundings
to the ears
of their hosting hearts;
and the pace of their furnishing
is a dark peace,
companioned of a grey fragrance,
pungent so that
it pierces as ebony tears, incising:
the inside heart brought to outside, shadowed
light,
still a finesse of the hidden,
and, into an ill banishment,
all true laughter, the white hart leaping,
a dull fancy.

***

"The ending of longing…inside…," a penning,
true, from my reservoir of sentiment,
finding thoughtful awareness,
my mourning, my constancy in kneeling
at the feet of yesterday.
And I knew, for the moment of the dewdrop,
that I had, in the larger portion,
made my prison, and in the
small courage of vacillation, the
agony of looking and saying, of
not looking and not saying, I choose to remain there, for life is more
in contrast, the consort of pain giving over to
small and grande fulfillment, his arm
offered, once and more, to begin again.

***

the stone of insight is heavy;
I am pulled along by my thought,
and I cannot, now, take and lead

***

Perhaps the cur that spars with my heels
is out climes of the politic chemical;
or those philosophical, but more,
perhaps,
reluctant, accepting recognitions such as
the only partial reality of flowers,
of loves, yesterdays and tomorrows—
all within eternal silence, audible to me,
eternal, covering all.

***

And what was, is but in shadow,
and what is coquettes with wished illusion.
Lines, and the messages they draw, are
tenuous, if only wished true; and all is
open to perused speculation.

***

—the great paradox of individual self,
the goal of all prologue, joining the
ever all, the true essence of each,
our risings up, or lyings down.

***

To toil, and feel warm, labored breath and it
to fall onto the wet of shoulders and brow
is noble, good—and in reflection—
appears in lovely hues, but hallelujahs
metamorphosing into words of freedom
and exclamations, to the tender tones of caresses:
sundown loses a portion in us,
but it, must as much, smiles on
fancy and colors, touch and secrets
that can become as bread, leavened.

***

I would a bell to ring and its echo answer
across all time, and I would bow,
with a portion of joy, that the
echo's sound was that of voice to me.

***

Another perhaps: my mother, in the darkness
of me in her belly, ate the herb of bittersweet
burking the joy I feign or tenuously hold;
but death was even yet in love, for she, when there
was no choice, yet with choice, would not purge
but conspired to hold up her own, a haunting,
saddened melody that would join the singing of
those their sorrow, or fuller, sing for some who
could not, whose sorrow is that of all, the blossom
which offers memory of that now which was, but,
as light passes, leaving suggestion of the real to our
fancy—the memory of that which could, not to perish,
but to reward all thought, which, of such seeking
does, and will reach forward its continuing
beauty.

***

I believe that I may die in a ditch of unknowing,
I of truth and other, and they of the whole of me.
It may be that I threw
the first stone and, rather, should
have walked away into benevolent
ignorance and therefore provided belief.

***

the bending of the spirit is painful,
manifesting sweetest, beyond that imagined,
sorrowful beyond full comprehension.

***

That terrible moment when the lighted
match blooms the fragrant candle—
the full noxious before the truly beautiful:
how so our days—

***

Sweet touch—exquisite silence; a raindrop
the true ecstasy of covering grace,
its guise, beautiful, filling mystery—
yet a season—all only a moment:
in their remembrance, only, lies their eternity.

***

Cobblestones and horses hoofs, the summer
silence in obscurity of the falling apple; the
continuous giving up of blossomed beauty—
let me see through, often and more, the window of my
closed, yet captured study. Scales are heavy and wound
as they fall away; the dark is safer, familiar, but, oh
my soul, light is.

***

This thread embraces me so that I am more at one with myself,
inclusive of all others, beside—the thread of golden
thought that twines throughout the all of our souls—

***

I, at times, do not know if I pursue, without
choice, or I am, of my own knowing, still
without choice, the pursued.

***

Summer Paths

In truth, so sweet, alongside the poverties
of the very beauty of days given beyond the
hearts of babes,
the countenance of youth,
the fuller wisdom
in pain.

***

Violets and lilacs—lovely, sweetly romantic—
to all who see them, in physical presence or in thought;
perhaps, we all see them, always, through
the instruction of our responses to them,
yet we, in our absence to their fragile flesh of petal
and fragrance—O, theme of our most well spoken
bard—these very shadows of our place for a time,
a season with them.
A sadness in the relief of knowing—

***

The day is, now, in apology after the
noon hour, and
silver lights in the heavens suggest
a sterile cold.
The clock need, then, send no message of
the hour, for tense is fluid and is
always flowing into those
portions that lie in the away.

***

Time held is awkward to its offspring
and brother, the present,
and
time, stilled, is death to all that it
attended and dressed.

***

—genzine and absinthe, bitter flowings of healing;
love and loss, bitter hewings of heavy wisdom.
Afterthought—or perhaps, moreso, the given,
prologue into finale—

***

I thought of other worlds and possible
living manifestations of the all Being,
to come in thought to fancy that flowers
and leaves, the abundant sky,
the sea and shore—all were
dancing colors given music, fragrance,
and knowing; and as they imaged
all that they surveyed, they
quieted, to then bath the tired, and
weep the sad; they poured out
themselves upon the sill and danced
in frolic with the gay;
most I imagined that they bound their
images, all, in their every extending
flowings—

***

As the leaves trembled, just outside
my window, I, in thought which
knew a reverence, bided
the absolute great held in
caught simplicity.

***

Life is a clever tryst into which we are thrown,
of chance or plan, no matter;
we may lie in it, or weep in it,
and breathe deep passion into it;
but always, always, we are in the own of it,
where passion and signs drop off as golden
leaves, crimson leaves,
finishing their mysteriously dark, prescribed
season.
Adolescent sentiment as in R. Frost, in his beginning work;
I cannot mature past regret.

***

Oh, find me, embrace me, hide me
sweet desert, of your solitude;
I implore Thee to come to my desperate
need of Thy healing, unwalled hospice.

***

memory finds always in summer, the engulfing,
smothering waves of heat, embroidered
with gardenia fragrance;
metaphor splendid, and of these glory,
the passion of first love,
always a summer, a radiance that must
find its diming but closeting its flame
in the deep wells, covered of fern and moss,
waiting the grey, the tremulous smile of fidelity,
its pastels against flame and
gold.

***

How sweet the truly beautiful;
how bittersweet the whole of the truly
beautiful.

***

Providence, the benevolent grantor,
circumstance and will, allowed;
time, the elixir:
and beauty, stained of pain and loss, in joy—
an insightful awareness which
catches the hand to the throat—

***

Awaking suddenly after short sleep,
and being aware of the coming
morrow, daybreak and consciousness—
these offerings—
a moving, yes provocative reminder of the gift
of life: all in the quiet of the night and
the moon,
knowing her willed, necessary death—

***

Melodies conclude
I am consumed with thoughts of death, of every
fashioning; I cannot bear the night, but the
day offers only mementoes to what can even be.

***

The day has been all of itself, now into closing,
just as all other days which have gloriously
arrived into their passing loss.
A path behind that fills up with dark as it increases
to the fore, leaves the fanciful romance of yesterday;
and out beyond, lies a way interminable, having no
harbor, no port, only the certain darkness gathering
from behind, to each into conclusion against all
fable and legend, but true, from the lips of none,
the silent.
How to bear the wealth inside the knowing of emptiness:
out happenchance, to which it will come to fall.

***

The moment, any moment, can be known fully,
only in its afterwards.
Reflection is powerful, the strength
of freedom in the lifting flight of a thousand doves;
but the moment of its calling cannot be bested, either
by
sentiment, reason, or repeated senses of
passion; it is alone in its holding.
In these paradoxical knowings lie a paramount sorrow of all hearts.
Thenso—
"The fealty of my heart remains within the lost."

***

I wish a carriage, or a splendid horse,
and should these not find to take
me beyond the spill, I wish
wings or a friendly apparition
that would walk with me
into light, without height or parameters
at all, but in unsounded
words be memory only, of the
side left before.

***

I am teased through the day by hope—
but in the night, its beacons dim, and at first
consciousness, although grateful that light has
been left for me, hope is near silence, more again
and must be coached, courted again—
sometimes, and I do not know just whyso,
a tiring charade.

***

Everything in my fancy, guarding against loneliness,
is open-ended, extant, but not fully real,
a lost romance, but affording life—therefore
the possibility of that not ever before dreamt.

***

Oh God, I am a quivering child inside,
a thoughtfully troubled, ageless self outside,
looking in.
Cover me in mercy with Thy coat of
many colors, a sweet fair linen, the sunlit
swan-cloud that drifted away from its
blue.

***

I left the chimney at Pineview, the bright
nasturtiums behind it, the blue morning-glory
by the gate, the fuchsia oleander to the right
of the bamboo fence—
I left them all and forgot them—
and, in this moment, I have caught them back
again.
Sweet are once traveled roads that come close again.

***

Part-Song

Come, come now to me; free my hands,
quicken my steps; back the twilight
to my waist, Thy purpose
rise inside my house of giving.

***

These tiny charms evoke sentiments akin
to honor, a regality, a rich presence,
a rare treasure
to grace the coming
of my new day, a new consciousness,
a furthering of soul—
let my steps be as the roses, discovered
yesterday at twilight, flying into my
heart and sealing fast.

***

Sunlight, moonrose, my song, my song,
before you sing into the wind;
a manuscript of feeling is waiting into telling.

***

Inside raindrops are kingdoms, fiefdoms,
palaces, courts, and opulent boundaries whose
spaces are the seats of dreams woven
by purist light.

***

the dirge of tense sounds loss and recollection, only,
it to fly away, if slowly, into the
vaulted hall of yesterday and tomorrow, the first
hours of poor mead, of the enigma
of all sense and thought, breath and
touch—the living left over
of dying experience—

***

HolyfatherGod, fashion me again, with the
loveliness of balance and objectivity,
saving me whole in the
center of Thy hands,
Thy porcelain doll, faint for
life and in life.

***

HolyfatherGod, that we find happiness in
a safe place, the beautiful dark, lighted
garden where Thy doll
may count the petals to all her flowers.

***

let me lie in the warmth of your season, one summer
glorious, and free into you, my breath,
become still and sweet.

***

There are, then, fallen hours in the day, and, in
clouds and clouds of very silence,
in my very heart,
it almost as a stain which does not
schedule, only, between failing
night and breaking day.

***

—reality before the still, watchful silence
These moments, together, take my days

***

—Under a very umbrella of depersonalization, a
desperate moment, to pass I think, as always,
leaving a darkened wound, a heavy atmosphere
that will dissipate until the next time—

***

We cannot forget the day,
though it becomes altogether
the night.

***

Every exchange or manipulation is not a Rose.

***

baked sweet potatoes after three o'clock, cold, drying
mud puddles, poor spider-webbing—and dirty cement
sponsoring time, past—cover them quickly, willsome
drape, for they are real, with no charms or dreams to dress them—
a slow, purposeless afternoon—necessary for rest, yet
stifling in its unrequiring, without warmth; but
to vanquish an innocent—
(The Stranger, Camus)

***

VERSES

We speak in softer tones when the time
is of the moon, and before shadows
fully clothe their portions;
night birds will come to silence,
presently, and left will be
only the nightingale to sing her lament
of roses.
Night forgives, but in her fullness, casts
deeper care upon selected hearts;
a candle, a lamp, the slightest
light of new dawn is remembered,
antidotes to sorrow that
fill up the dark, it having
vanquished all innocent light.
Death is in life, life is in death;
selection is, in part, our own,
but acceptance is all that is
our own when players of night best
our efforts though we yet, armed with able
antidotes, and more
when day does not arrive fair.

***

And as I rise, with Thee, my staff,
with Thee, my sandal,
to walk my work,
to make the joy Thou hads't
set in portions before me,
thanks be to God.
Amen
The almost constant scourge of grey, motionless
illness does not now touch me.
Thanks be to God.
Amen

***

—sentiment apart from my usual worship at the feet of yesterday, but today, somehow, yesterday is only a reminder of the issues in being, if sometimes embellished to comfort and even deny.

***

The beauty of a bird's lifting,
the hope in sunlight on tall autumn tree barks;
the joy in forgiveness and grace,
the peace in a glance toward twilight
—moments, the only traversing the span of time
to the heart;
words that capture merely catch
afterglow, and like echoes,
are true,
but truly after, and not within.

***

Ah reason, against all fable, but true, lying
against the heart, marry thee together that
we not despair in moments of loneliness,
of ease, when dreams taunt us with images
of what has been and what can be, that space
between knowing and holding; these moments
do come, like beautiful maids in waiting, paused
to their lady, gifting her fan, lifting her hand,
offering arms and warmth, strength and
condolence, ushering in moments, all the more
generous, if poignant, in their ephemeral
properties.

***

Inside my first awareness, I want to run to you,
run to you, to chronicle the night when you are
not there, except in beautiful, unworded and knowing
assurances—to speak of adventure in the coming
day—when laughter and all good play about.
—But most, to know, again, once again that you are,
and in our fashion, you are with me, beside me in touch
and smile, and understanding, across the miles reality
strews out, but close in sentiment, gardenia sentiment,
early summer warmth, sentiment that is ever within.

***

no, no, not my ring; the dolls, the dolls
are nearer now, an echo around my
being, sifting through my
troth with myself, to my core,
for in their silence there is not even memory
of ringing, or any sound, but only
the peace of nothing;
until their strength wanes and
I again, struggling with wakefulness,
remember rings, no not, no ring.

***

HolyfatherGod, the pathos of the present
beautiful—the heavy motif, the melon's
heart; the tip of the candle flame,
sensual blush against wisdom's pale,
and, coming, autumn's wealth—
these to only become beautiful past,
it, then, to can be held:
I could leave it, crush the dewdrop
into still water, but this present
beauty if, in truth, prerequisite, is aperitif,
to other more, an explained,
kindly absinthe.

***

And I will sleep again,
most,
that Thou art,
and in Thy warrior voice will come to me
in the legend I have, and do
pen,
out the yearnings of my
heart:
with thought of Thee, I will sleep,
copper lights among Thy feathers,
a touch of gentle
laughter,
these grooming me
as I lay me
down.

***

Where unto do I fly; where in this furthest
afterwards is the path.
Will the violin bow transport me
or will the trumpet lift my now grey soul.
The organ points my spirit, but the will and
strength to blessing are bent and
inertia is a pall that falls over
me—
except the memory that once, even now
just a touch, I wished, and
in brightest fancy of the gift of
first days,
I saw the butterfly in the sun, the
firefly in the moon, and a
passionate radiance caught me up in
their/its glow.
There was thought of only reaching, catching,
and holding, past any time of seasons.
There were chariots filled with

mornings, and baskets of touch
and knowing.
Paths rolled out like the highwayman's
ribbon and bejeweled moments
spread over them all.
But now the paths, and their seasons of fatigue and
convenience, have become all the same,
and I am spent with hedgerows,
heather, the yonder heath, yet the knotted thicket, the limberlost.
Show me a simple, unadorned, but true lane,
which leads to the far pasture.

***

Given to me, then, was a gift I cannot
have in waking hours, but the ever
clever, and today, kindly,
yearning keeper of my heart was
accepted by my thought;
and
I have memory of all of Thee,
Thee, most splendid, resplendent only unto me,
and I, with thy beauty,
in queenly radiance.
HolyfatherGod,
pour out my bones, full of will;
gentle the wind, just the
tint of lilac,
and I will stand, I will
stand,
and the wind, even of
yesterday and the veiled tomorrow,
it will pass, into my
rest of before; the now of thought,
and beyond.

***

The existential tease—the clever, even
insidious deceit that has taught
my lessons into its own;
and in the loathing of it in
my whole,
my constant exclamations and
lamentations drawing
truth as my own—I have been,
ever now these most recent seasons all, hunted
by my own knowing, and I am, in
these moments of pain, unthinkable,
struck, my shouting, will ignited, balming
autumn wine, and fatigue of
strong wind—these diverting my attention,
and no sacrament to my hands,
I am struck to the mark, and in my own
blood,
my beautiful scarlet, saved and
saved,
to stand against this wind, in this my gathering blood.
I cannot knowingly speak.
*** November 9–10, 2002
Separated from all and everything.
I walk in an unreal dream where my toys seem even strange to me,
now, my thoughts almost an exercise. I am trapped, for reasoned
loyalty and love to Mamma and Daddy, and anger and pride against
others; I cannot die; but there is death possible without dying.
I was given great wealth, but my illness has
taken the greater part—my sweet,
innocent passions, elusive peace, finding the true
absurdity of happiness, trust, truth.

***

I rose at seven, and the November light
was beginning its manifest;
I bent to light a candle, and my glance fell
to the small November light,
poised, through French door windows,
on the rug—ah, how poor the light we
mortals can make.
And as I walked out, presently, at the very moment
of my looking up, large limbs, cut away
and caught into fuller, live trees—they, dead
and heavy,
left their clasp of two weeks' felling, and crashed
to the ground.
The space left gave up light which caught
my silver, haloed by celestial newness
in the echoing silence—
I was beautiful as a second red, yet wet scarlet,
geranium that had entered out of season
during the night's forbidding cold.
In a moment's suddenness, reflection
swiftly pierced my awareness, and I knew
that I was in a moment; I was alive,
and everything that was, was alive in me.
The muse had come unnoticed and unpetitioned
to my shoulder, and sat like a colossal blossom,
heavy in its own profusion, stamens of bronze, and
copper with pistils of diamonds washed
of knowing gold, to fall away as
the beautiful dancing light of worded thought.
Songs then—and colors pouring out suns and moons,
yet myriad stars of feeling—
plume of grace, touch my fingers as they speak,
my thought in moments, hours, days,
coming.

***

In looking back through earliest morning
hours, the imaged night was
found kind,
for it had passed with queenly
quiet,
taking a portion of hurt with it.
Distance rolled out,
and voice withdrew, and perhaps,
almost as a condolence,
memory, running with its generous basket
of filling gold, lost, quiet
with an innocence,
the particulars that wounded,
but kept together those which
are sweet.
The oldest knowing began its serpentine spiraling,
pushing upward toward defenseless
consciousness,
the soul aware, where the sparring of
will and the jury come, of
timeless speaking, this knowing, fatigued
of constancy's integrity,
kneading, baking,
pressing the grape all new
in a new day.
Old in its familiarity, absurd,
even into hopeless
sentiment,
coming woundings, loss not to be caught
back,
but shadowed by fire of attending
passion's smile, weaving,
in the strength of contrast, a
shroud of incredible beauty, the

very grief in a basket
of filling golden pears,
known, held, of their rapture
touched,
to must release and give order to the
purposed pressing of sound and fury,
a tale told by the dying unable.

***

The cathedral stands grande and imposing,
and its shadow, like its afterthought;
likeso stands early the day,
grande and imposing, its moments
of sand and mortar, air and sunlight
passing through;
ought to do is to walk through the corner-
stones, the lines broken, straight
and fair, the bramble
of thought and feeling embracing
the grandness and the imposition:
the cathedral is always beside its afterthought
as the day is beside its yesterday.

***

Cold, January raindrops, falling, falling
to the earth, one by one;
day breaking over all creation,
slowly, slowly, tree by tree;
and moments, sounding constantly,
constant into my consciousness, passing away,
away.
These hold within my thought the ephemeral
nature of being, yet my heart is
long and long, through yesterday
into tomorrow, with a sweetness that
nourishes beginnings and their
conclusions.

**

—but lost, to wander into the wind, as to be caught
in desperate wishful reaching,
into a mourning, even that
whose face of grief flows out beyond
description,
and in acquiescing to the dark moon,
torn out, scattered, the wind-touched
thistle, my struggling personhood,
my round of design with flaw
or any that prepared or executed false,
I, to lie under heaven's benign, yet pity of fury.

**

The Early Spring Garden
Morning

I do not wish to forget the small, early garden, seen
today, on Davis Road, and my memory of Daddy,
only Daddy and his gifts to me. How pressing the hurt that so many
of them cannot ever be mine again: so great was my weeping,
for miles and miles.

The Early Spring Garden
Night

His words I held, from the years of their
first giving, but in the poignancy of
the half-dream,
his face shown as a sacred relic,
kissed, and filled of its blessing;
but more, keeping in the memory that,
with careful immediacy, caught into the image,
it shining, surely,
as Trinity Presence,
four in divinity, increased of recorded
three, not usurping Divine order,
but only therein invited,
to certain my abiding,
in love and care,
complete.

***

Flower my voice and the contours of my face,
that my gathering be the berry full,
and of passionate hue granted.
And good could have left its holding
theory, eloquent: cast aside, to in love
be loved,
a becoming of threads that,
as evening vespers,
bind into righteousness, faithfulness,
and
speaking wisdoms, elegant and grey,
these, together, declaring
the shadowed fable of truth.

***

In all the dark of your farewelling
I sat and then I stood, only
to sit again; your voice
just sounding,
was past, leaving me in a
motionless solitude.
And all my angels now have
satin of silver, silver quilted to a muted
grey;
and all the clouds above wander
now, like torn petals of
virginal purity,
etched about and slightly
dusted of a silent ash;
and winds of late summer

are idyll breath, hanging
as generous folds of
clouded gauze;
and the young harlot's perfect
lips
parted,
as feigned—her
heart offering
songs
of blackberries;
my hand came to
my heart, my throat,
and
it brought all
the dark
with it, the dark
of your
farewelling.

***

I am a flower that, in a great portion am full in my separate own,
but who dies in my lack, more throws off dead
brown, lying beside truths and
yesterday's recollections, for strawberries
dress in scarlet, and do not grow, cannot grow
in desert places.

***

I have an old sadness around me
just now, as I waken to the day,
one that has been with me,
a companion of long,
familiar,
visitation.
In its silence, I hear time lost,
and feel the pain
of its useless left;
there is no hour, there is no day,
but only the season of passing,
from which apparitions of beauty
and good
drift by with their unknowing
mortality.
Can awareness don a hue,
a sound, a form—then it is
this knowing I house within,
grey and silent, and covering, a pall of
emptiness and reflection of that
out which it issues.
For yesterday is the child of tomorrow,
today, its wetted birth, drying,
and the glory in these infant moments
are truly only exquisitely,
lovely
weepings.

***

We forget, yet we remember, in stances different
with the years; and in moments of quiet,
in seasons of special significance,
images visit in their real and metaphorical
forms, having metamorphosed, but also having
kept the heart's own.
The stage remains the same, for we live yet,
if between different props, but the
players, the script and its scenes continue to
arrange around the deeper parts
of ourselves; so ought to do is but to catch
the beggar coins that fall from their purse,
and hope that they add beauty to the afternoon.

***

Through—

Through the lighted window,
a moth fluttering;
through the lighted window,
day, in the dark,
breaking;
in the candle flame, memory,
dying, into speaking
through another flame,
another dark;
through early morning's
window, Easter morning.
As it came tough this time—

***

Like moving, golden goblets, filled with wine,
red and lighted, graced with cherries of summer
radiance, less their wetted
Mediterranean shadows—
the Grande Femme of humanity dances,
en masse, so that all are in motion,
and only those inside the teapot know.
I moved, from seed, to bud and flower, but I, most
a lesser god, would see beyond, in and out
rhythms, sound, and metamorphosing steps;
I continued to move, an impossible
season, the force of need for a kingdom seating
me upon the horse of complacency,
mundanity, but I continued, still, to look
about and see.
Dissonance came to usurp the decorated chair
of patience, and there began, what seemed, almost
not, but all the faintest glow of the emerald
moth of the limberlost.
I glimpsed the growing magnificence of its hue,
and the goblets grew into silence, falling
among their own splendid, spilled nectars.
Was it apparition or merely the known reality
of the hour past noon—in that lonely
moment of ever—that I knew the flame;
and whether in vaunted hubris, or its residual
self-hate, I saw the flame, and wept, with moans
and bending, that it was.

***

great cycle down, all day—
I have been more and more in dissociation,
so that now I lie a helpless charge of flesh,
without identity or purpose;
I do not know my features, and awareness is strange to me;
I know and I do not know,
so long this path.
Illness of troubled fancy leave me with words only,
voicings out a well of troubled dark waters,
still, yet.
The intense pain in my hands both anchors and
estranges me, for I want it away, apart,
caught and saved into containment
outside me, but saved, to feed these later,
the anchoring to a strange, beautifully
frightening reality.
My own chemistry, awakened, more than
of the poppy,
the mushroom,
or ancient grasses—

***

I can smell the dark the hear the quiet
and I know the inside of being,
for there are seasons of thought
and feeling, of steps and holding, of
insights and beauty, with the
unpleasing beside.
These are seasons of strength and
dreaming, in long days of sunshine and
rainfall; there are seasons of truth
and justice, mercy and forgiveness
covering over seasons of hurt
and loss.

Sunshine and winds, flowers and
and open sky, and water; mountains
housing temples and singing chimes
circumference seasons for those whose
yearnings carry them into these pastures.
—But knowing the inside of being is to see
conclusion and there are none
who escape this horse of
routing, and we all know
bittersweetness as we mount.

***

The Pause

O marvelous, simplicity and
the splendid, woven into my complex
waking routine,
always from sleep at different night hours, a
single awareness or a broken continuing, as a potion
drying up. After each pouring,
joy alive in its loss:
to know, in review, the complete grief
of night, its pirating of thought
and movement,
yet beauty decorated with half-truth
and dark, clothed images;
—to wander through these such paths
and arrive into day, into thought
and will,
this circumstance brings, yea,
the careless unbeliever
to humble pause.

***

I, supposed if I burn as fire, I, yet, cannot be consumed, snuffed;
my logic fathered in the heat of my
passion;
I cannot know another; and loneliness
burns away my hope and resolve; fancy
dances around my head as the Medusa's
ringlets, alive and writhing,
promising poisoned rapture in their ruby eyes—jeweled
and hungry fangs.

—Give my tenderness back to me, the leaf, the
morning's bloom, smiles and words heavy
with the wisdom of searching.
For when the room is closed, and it is filled
with darkness, only, mere myths whisper,
and we, in nothing but shadow-flesh, eat left over
berries of the lost morning, and
gather, sweetly, blossoms whose cheeks are pressed,
fatigued, to our shadow selves.

—Let me hold my tenderness a moment more, before it
frees in the night, having burnt out its light
in useless fury. The sound is silence, touch
is lost, imprisoned in the pungent chrysanthemum's
moment passed. Our shadow flesh drifts into
the night with the sentiments of
our shadow hearts, which grieve that our passion
burned with such fervor so that it consumed the inside
sweetness, of yesterday, of now, and the darkened
highway suddenly becoming the taker of
all truth, the all of having been.

For even when lost, it is the close familiar that is loved and remembered
and the bursts of passion become empty images except for their
diming auras of exciting.

—Strange thoughts with a kind of rage at the tiring ordinaire,
but fear to not keep the familiar.

***

Jeweled Apples

We open obediently to the day, our steps finding
familiar paths, gathering haste with
laughter thrown out,
catching the sunlight;
music, of hope resting on the bed of forgotten
themes we always know,
makes sweet the wind that reminds our breath,
and we see small flowers
in our glances to window and door, these
appearing as with their latches open,
and, as in days passed, inviting.
And our apples fall about us, almost of chartreuse,
surely sweet confections, and holy crimson, to arrange in patterns
beautiful, as poetry of the feminine;
we do not hear them fall, neither review
or gather, in their familiarity, catching
moments of fatigue to the day.
Yet when the night, and the music, a dirge of bittersweet
Remembrance, sings out, we intuit that surely there was a season
when lovely apples fell, rare jewels
in their now absence, in their fancied
recollection—
it is become then a burden, of moments' unbearing,
that we know, but do not know;
and when wisdom guides us back,
into the music of lost gardenia,
we do know, with poignancy past all
understanding,
that we could never know our moments
in their immediacy, but with innocent,
into thoughtless disregard, let them die to remembrance,

safer there, perhaps, while we chased charming
bubbles which somehow
flattered our vanity and could not truly
touch our hearts;
always, in full, licensed deceit, empty, lifting beyond
any solace, they progressively join the full
meaninglessness of our steps, becoming
a true fancy, no more than an unfashioned,
full-waking sleep.
This wisdom, to know of lost moments, when
jeweled apples fell, their charming songs
of completed beauty mostly unheard,
these moments known, the hurting wisdom.

***

absinthe kisses
as petals leave their center, to fall to the below;
as raindrops move out their clouded
whole,
as individual tears, to slip into downward green,
or as the grape, fully round and
of color and meat most pleasant—in
this heaviness departs its vine
to join its sponsor, the very earth,
hearth to all seekers:
as these, with my every thought, my heart can but
let blood sentiments flow into the away,
for to linger past recognition,
they would use up their provided vessel,
of their growing pain, and hurt would
have no exiting avenue; and yet, unlike
the earth, which receives its bounty,
to be reassembled and enjoyed again, the nonexiting

flow would, of lips crimson,
mauve and wine gold, reds, rose—
flesh, and fuchsia,
consume their own true walls.
—thoughts in,
holding, thoughts flowing out, farewelling:
my recognition in certain, unforgiving moments,
dies, as absinthe kills, with every kiss.
I am strong only in yesterday, weary in today
and in tomorrow, in denial alone.

***

Give me some antidote—a flower,
a sound, a memory—
or better, perhaps, a lapse in
conscious thought,
a respite complete;
for I have wandered many paths, together
in dolls' indulgence, seeking this
such,
and in it lies a sweet portion, if
to fall away in unpleasant
return, but a peace enough to continue.
I do not know if I were in the freer consciousness,
but I intended peace, and this image came to me,
just as I awakened, so to pen, just as it came.

***

—Pouring over me warm, good, wisdom
in hues of love and faith, smiles
of summer lilies, and
fragranced about in every season, noble,
poignant sweet olive:
lost, but kept forever, being borne away
on winds that part only to always, ever
must return—
In the deepest night waters issue out silent
conversations,
whispered words from my beggar soul:
sweet ruminations, as honey mead ever was,
petitions as worthy as my heart can
offer,
and from the mountain, dreams verbalized,
those resting in pensive moments
and truest need.

***

Bramble, bramble, bright and dark,
whose outer twines, alone, we see;
inside, beyond description, disorder
and sorrow, but of good intent
its unraveling an outflowing stream
of peace and beauty,
truths whose lives live out into
the ever.

***

In a finesse as old as time, the morning
came in, past the full dark, the widening, certain
light, the shadows—more, the silence, the long
quiet that hung like a wetted wool cape about
my thought.

***

Oh, HolyfatherGod, give me Thy voice, if in presence
alone. Thy touch, Thy knowing of me
that I not perish of the visitation of none, or perish me quickly
if I cannot be
in Thy acknowledgement:
a soul—if worthy to Thee alone, whose fingers of grace can mercifully
lift or crush.
Beautiful dreamer,
I am not anymore afraid to die, most to live in emptiness,
alone, forgotten, dreams forever in the webbed net,
tangled bramble of time past.

***

Come, come tender moments, into every day
in each its seasonal holdings
that
I remember and be nourished as surely as
the beauty of existence
within a world of troubled thought and
doing.
With the potato, the fish, wheat, and grape—

***

Ah, golden black panther, sleek within
muscles breathing in and out,
across and between,
a queen's almond-shaped emeralds
in searching glints
from thy furtive, seeing space—
thee,
an occasional visitor, in sometime's
fancy, is, there disguised in thy appearing,
for constancy's pacings
are close to my core, searching, panting
for relief.
Panther, panther, in golden black, inside,
inside, holds a heart of brightest red;
as fresh, flayed meat;
it is wounded, and pacing moves
about the pain, with accompanying
hope for new space
of relief.
I walk with thee, tonight, in reverie, tomorrow
in small dramas and unworthy pathos,
in the marketplace and in
my finding solitude, dead steps all
about yesterday, for inside, I am
black gold, surely the prisoner thou art,
pacing, panting, breathing the pain
of the knowing captive, the trapping, the
capture, the tightening bramble
so distant as to be forgotten, under the
pain; but within the trap—real and without
understanding or knowing peace
out or from it.

Only when the muscles lie silent, flat,
without their supple firmness,
then will the gold, in content, its composition,
then it will,
a moving halo—widen, to spreading,
and lift, as the God-Man
Himself, transfigured
in light, through light, to be light in peace.
The golden black panther, an image from German
literature that often haunts my thought.

***

Morning Notes
Stanza Two
Summer, oh summer, mysterious notion
of long, golden quiet, lying within
its incense, bruised of warmth,
a lovely time of painted, wandering
clouds, without hours;
the fabled ship, which of its longing,
finds its moment the whitened
thistle, fully round, in flawless composition,
resting on tenuous stem, leaning
upward, but in its very person, when
reached for by eager hands,
although with careful hunger, its fragile
design, as if struck by force of
intense light, leaves its self, lifting
into profusion, as of our days, flying away
into its only store, that of recollection
and resigned weeping,
over all whichever was ours:
waiting, abiding accepting.

***

I lay on friendly linens and let the
music fall on me; I made confession,
admitting, I grieved, and
I was full of thanksgiving.
In these days I know truth which I lay
aside throughout all the other seasons;
the fire burned and hurt
in its ashes, cavalier, but memory
knows, still, the pleasure
of its flame.
It was, it came to be, and it was, O then;
and the rain of a thousand days
will not wash away the knowing
of the troth, the loss of it, and its
finding again in coming,
final ashes, out of season.
On hearing Foster and Allen in early morning rain.
Remembering, December 15, 1992
Date of Richard's death

***

sisters, sisters you know the flow of my thought, my faithful dolls,
come quickly now. I do not wish to know of your power, only
the complete nothing that it graces into my tired spirit.
and oblivion has become as a holiday, with pleasant expectancies
and contentment entering my senses: gentle hue of dark, quiet
sounds of silence, the peace of rest,
the petal of rose, the wet of dew, the gold of first day—all are more
beautiful, but they cannot be summoned at will—and my will is
tenuous, wanting, fatigued, so that my call goes out unevenly through
fully constant moments.
oh, for the petal, the dew, the sunrise: perhaps my sisters, true, after
their boon of absent thought, perhaps—for even the gods wake to
a new day.

***

Throughout these southern climes, forests,
and smaller, darker wood, sing melodies of
cascading yellow jasmine blossoms, in
profusion of childhood memory: relics, these,
brought out and seen, again, to, with the
wisdom of rebirth, and silence, for they come
quickly to shadow, whisper on the wind, to be
taken away among embraces which bind them
to moments passing of glory, into collection,
of hours and record.
These lie in innocent sleep, their sighs reaching
out of yesterday, but they lie in a prescribed
peace, and all that before, and more, that beyond,
we color into pastel gods and goddesses, czars
and czarinas, kings and queens, with their lords
and ladies, the company of the highborn whose
buckles and fans, and jeweled hairpins we dream,
perchance, to catch, at their falling, and return;
—fancy, of great strength and ableness, so that
we do not remember our loss of honeysuckle, or
where it is, what it might become—
"A leaf, a stone, a door."
—Thomas Wolfe

***

The Mirroring

In fullest consciousness, my sudden waking
found a wall of silence, that of the
fallen hours.
Those of the birthing morning,
its travail without voice,
but speaking as a torrent of images
surging about,
a very floodwater of festival and
memory, into the halls of yesterday.
And I do not wish to journey there, to wander
among the voice of my solitude,
its quiet bittersweet, its insistent
absences
which dress with emptiness, certain chambers of
my heart.
To paint out shadows, to allow echoes to die;
to sound chimes with bells, to press
old flesh—in these would find mortal
my solitude,
but, in these, almost, without a saving reprieve,
these chambers of absence would
fragment and fall away,
leaving me, in greatest truth, less;
and so I must, beside my laughter, provide
a mourning, that the whole of me
leap forth, full awake today, to stay its
hours,
left holding, given, imaged in form and fragrance,
the rose, nourished by its own
emptying, mirroring the full bittersweet.

***

I lay in the dark, hearing the violin's concerto,
saying love within beauty of pleasant, but unknowing
company, the music the beauty of sanguine fellows,
the nightwind the love in your eyes.
And the dark wrapped me in its arms, close, and
featherlike tender, the gentle ambiance of the moment
near to a small, quiet ecstasy.

**

Great Thanks
Great thanks into the still wind,
the long day out of beautiful morning,
growing ever to be more,
into the quiet goodbye of gentle chill
and sunset in carnival hues of orange and red,
lying across the wideness of generous sky
like the unspeaking violin string,
full of its silent speaking,
my heart the invisible bow;
but great thanks, still;
yet more,
for new beginnings, without the hurt of first,
violent rupture,
or memory that brings it,
in its fullness, again:
—great thanks, still, yet.

**

—Flow, and let be the power of camaraderie,
a touch of acquaintance well
sought, the love of
those whose tenses do not matter,
but only their sweet
constancy:
invaluable winds bearing fragrance
into thought when I am
alone,
…alone in sweet captivity of my
rooms—
—thoughts throughout the night, even as I painted;
presence above, being alone, camaraderie, a
thousand gifts of thoughtfulness—

***

Gracious Dissonance

I listened to Mamma, I wept with Mamma;
I carried my father in my arms
as I looked forward, to see the faces of my
brownskins, leading them by my
voice.
The memory was a dream, and it was truth,
and my heart opened to accept it all;
I cleaved to the whole togetherness of the scene,
knowing such was a concept, precious,
taken away with the years, kept alive
in my heart, alone.
With a great fatigue issuing out of time,
the players were sought and held as rarest gems,
to tumble downward, and away into
yesterday.

Left is a gracious dissonance that let me know,
courting legend, that there was in my self
blood and wounds, beside lovely sentiment which
filled up my withered spirit: made, in this moment,
gloriously, full round and smooth, if with
bittersweetness of giving past healthy selfhood.

**

The night was still, wrapping me about
like a dark, flowing gauze;
its echoes of the past day were distant,
being pressed aside by new light,
coming.
And in silence, the bamboo's green flame
blew colorless in the late night wind.
Yet, I was with myself, yet and more,
that I was in company with thought,
a favorite sport, most, but always an exercise
in balance—
beauty against ill, dark after night is
done, spilling over the glory of
sunrise—
will I be, in weighing, able to see the
tender splendor beside the hound
which stalks, ever, to outdistance him, once
again.

**

I image the cello and violin,
hearing their voice;
I know distant, falling water
as silence that is audible, ever;
I remember sunsets more than
sunrises,
in sentiment, and earth tones
tumble over pastels and deeper, colorful hues.
The grande person of yesterday stands
against the vibrancy of
the moment—
what is wrong, what is wrong;
what has always been wrong.
Pour me into a clear, crystal bottle
and in the early morning
set it in the sun's smile.

***

I do not look anymore to find summer love,
that gathered among gardenia
and anointed on warm, soiled bedding,
that of impromptu excitements,
the sausage of experience
which fattens our musings with deepest melancholy
so that we may have our joy.
I do not anymore look after summer love,
for the love of these present days is one of acceptance
with a politeness, out of impotence;
there is no fire in the heart,
no crimson, no imagination
of what sleeved blows might accomplish.

May bedrooms, again arranged,
shout September touches,
and done so with skill,
and the linens are white,
starched with Christian industry;
great importance is in the colors
because the fire burns now by appointment,
precious ardor having been eaten away in many hungry days.
And so, we make fewer toasts,
and brandy is not so necessary.
Flowers of silk will do,
and when the old songs are heard,
we somehow think we know better now;
and anger might put into disarray the swans.

***

The Face

We all, each, walk the way,
with our sacks of stones,
our bundles of rags,
our tender handkerchiefs, filled
and tied, within
our closest sentiments.
And we, all, each, leave them, at different
receivings, they all, each, in our walk
along the way.

***

an Elizabeth afterthought—

The reference to the "tied handkerchief" is to an old behavior of our people in Mississippi (and probably other deep Southern states): that of tying (women, in the main), what few little coins they could gather together to "travel"—somewhere, anywhere. This custom was most seen, possibly more often, among our then called "black folk."

In my lifetime, really, my adulthood, I have seen the passing of this behavior, and uncomfortableness, and even anger at its mentioning (among some). I think it a "quaintly humble" characteristic of a period (gender, socioeconomic, and some other variables, interacting) in America's history, not to be forgotten, but recorded and reflected upon for further wisdom.

Today, we see individuals living under bridges and in shelters; our closest ancestors still show beggars, pickpockets as a trade, and other such like activities: the face of humanity does not change; it always favors the whole of itself. Humility need not be placed only in worshipful scapes.

**

Speaking Rilke, "build myself a [winter]," a season.
Surely, then, I could remember, and know,
experience and feel, quite without
the varied dissonances that are constant to me.
Ah soul,
beggar in nobility,
let me know,
let me feel that I am, clothed in solitude, hued of nothing,
yet in fancy and in my raw flesh, know the beauty of my full
humanity.
The closet will not wear, alone, and close,
nor the fair with its gatherings,
and open; somewhere, sometime,
there must come a ceremony,
a consented marriage.

**

My thought cannot stretch out more, for truth is
at my door; voices and movement are in a salad
of confusion and beauty, the flowers of the day losing
their smiles of brilliant yellow, red scarlet,
and vibrant rose within paled rose.
Push all away, and bring to me all silence; I am
as the slave lifter of Pyramid stones, weak in strength
of flesh and will, bearing sensitive to every stimulus,
too fatigued to respond, but to wrench towardward
an answer which tears my whole self, Usher and I.
I wish to hear the twilight fall, and night winds blow,
but the noise of emptiness, the leaving of pulling
out of myself, arranges but a clamoring over my toys.
My eyes cannot keep to see, my arms fall at limp
ease, my legs not to support; my thought grows dark.
And I beg touch, acknowledgement, acceptance
in warmth, and in company of peace.

***

—Four hours of night since the rain,
and the imagined huge limb, sounding
massive, crushing the already
fallen leaves, was down, from one of
the south trees.
In the dark I can only surmise that no structure
was touched, for the sound was heavy weight
falling, uninterrupted, to rest.
Now
that the rain is spent, the chime
unseemingly still in the light's small
casting,
the limb in repose, now all is at peace,
much as when I hear dogs barking in the
far distance, almost as playful exercises,
and, in rare moments the voice in song of he
who has become my owl dove.

In reflective peace, I am pulled aside to think of opposites,
drawn to darkened events; and like a reptile
striking, the bramble from its center, constricts,
grows tighter, out into a fixed curling of the individual
twines.
In moments close, I will see the limb, the dogs will
have quieted as the owl dove has flown.
The day will approach with its promise,
its fancies and woundings, its refuge
and its nakedness; there is no
certainty or fortress except in the thought,
the moment, and in all the dark
against the light, the right and good against
the most unaccepted—
the bramble is all of it and it houses,
in
necessities, our day.

***

When morning's dew sparkle had danced
away its hour, the cat has turned
into a princess,
the birds into elegant queens and
gentle ladies;
and bamboo reached with its most
upward touch, to catch and hold,
for a beautiful moment,
soft, ariel clouds which had
become snow-white calla, floating—
My heart sang these songs, and others, more,
into the dying of the day's firstness,
with a silent deferring to the
hour of noon, and the dutiful dénouement
of remaining day.
Now, in these finishing hours, if
fancy can play with nocturnal

gifts,
spiders will weave as concert masters,
bringing melodies of lace
for coming dews' embroidery;
sweet olive, bent in the warmth of full
sunlight, will become a splendid silver,
and whitest gold,
to know refreshment and send forth
maiden fragrance, adorned with
the very diamonds that smiling
stars can be.
And in that aftertime, moonlight, out which dreams
dress,
will find her dancers moving
with their lady, into shadow,
waiting faces dimming, but whose
movement becomes early
gold.
And so, there is no loss at twilight, or,
birth in daybreak, but rather,
to the seasoned ear and eye,
the hopeful, trusting heart,
there is a ribbon of grandeur, flowing
in, to out, to beauty and good,
a path for brief hours, in which to walk in bounty,
with a time/season resting,
the true hour of these,
their expected advent and epiphanies.

***

The night is lonely, for wheels are much
less in turning, voices closet inside
their chambers, yet the falling
leaf giving up its imaged song.
It is togetherness, the coming to find others'
sounds, that covers over whatever

loneliness is, to find entrance that night
affords.
There are paths to walk that ease the
emptiness, those of yesterday, of
tomorrow's waiting dreams, prayers that
fall a friendly drape, after blessing,
over those we love in every time.
As the lea lies laden
with its morning's sparkling dew, so
the bright of day lies out before us,
and bitter, bitter is the night
when, in its dress of dark, it does not
bring from the day the companion
of sweet contentment, the loveliness of
fatigue offering an abbreviated
peace.

***

In the quiet of early, lighting
morning,
I let a candle,
with honeysuckle in fragrance,
and watched the beginning,
infant flame,
small, and soft, in October chill.
It grew to leap upwards,
spreading light in more fullness,
a full coming sweetness,
and it caught the days,
all my days, and their dreams,
to flame for moments,
into the wide, empty
openness,
into the eventual
away.

***

Morning Notes
Stanza Three
"my own, my own"

In the mirror of new day, I find ashes
from a weeping fire,
a flower dying inside its radiance,
the rainbow fading, bleeding away
from its arc.
Morning promises, if they live beyond the
mirror's first drawing images, present a dew
of joy, but to fulfill in the
shadows of the day, small deaths
reminding;
and I must gather my hours into myself,
a daily harvest of egocentric mourning,
sorrow which cannot be forgiven,
but rather brought within again, of arms
whose fatigue, as amber,
lighted, knows its growing strength,
to be added to the dark that is our, each,
our accepted destiny, gardenia in
closing robes of deep umber,
sweetness becoming heavily pungent,
dressing, as with poetic feminine hand,
certain coming night.
Night sounds are beautiful,
a peace brought from childhood, before the
long journey began, a dark that
has given up light, but beside pain, arising from inescapable,
necessary rapture, but rippling out into great
wounding of one passenger, my heart.

***

Ah, Night

Beautifully moth-ladened and stained of the sensual, the
provocative—ah, night, mysterious wench, goblin- strumpet in
flowing, teasing dark, cockle the unwary, coquet the innocent,
and house your secrets, to show enough to trouble, yet parable
fears and forebodings as winds that blow constant.
I cannot come to thy loveliness, take thy hand encircled by the
moon, and tendered by the stars—not without terrestrial angst and
a wish for light which can put to rout all thy characters, shadowed.

A potion of the moonflower's ivory sweetness or early
summer's gardenia and honeysuckle in midnight's warmth,
together with the dividing—though elegant in
her farewelling—dark rose of midnight—these might embrace
such beauty as to please me some moments in the long
road of dreams, that I lie down in pleasant
pastures which still and restore.

***

Spring Eventide

Hesitating, eventide in soft pastel, but eventide
suddenly, and as a dreamer's wealth,
so likely hued.
Hours in patient gathering, truly,
those early and chilled,
into the quieting of first spring,
when the jousting of cold and
warmth was found under morning stars,
passed to the gradual event of the
silver lance acquiescing to that of gold.
The struggle and its accompanying moanings, its intense
pushing toward new flesh, or light and color
and touch—
these now show their prize of a remembered
harmony;

wooing and promises, in company of desperate
reaching, find their pause, the flower
open, its throat with warm blood of generous veins
spilling over to its petaled curls,
passion drawn full, as scarlet the butterfly,
a scarlet dove, the dewfall sparking
scarlet in new sunlight, lifting with their
ariel heaviness into their waiting,
journeyed ecstasy.
Passion beyond moaning into sighing and resting,
composed the beauty of using up, contentedly,
of confident knowing the circle whole
again, small intimacies forgetting small
wisdoms, discovering
sweet warmth, kisses, as stars from small
tiaras passed between,
fragrance and sounds, wind songs,
cloud and rain's Elvira
smiles, making fresh and eager, in the
sensual adventure of acquainted
hands:
passion in its being, brought by the eventide
of spring's joy, left in its echoes,
flowing into a golden dark,
a rich serenade opening toward the long
boulevard lighted by fireflies,
the long, long sweet summer's song.

***

Careful Execution

There is a tension and a waiting in all things,
a respectful pausing,
that speaking the wisdom of the second coming;
and when it is not acknowledged,
there is improper movement,
indistinct murmurings and unhappy flowing.

The sun enters, without ceremony, into violet,
and there appear violet tears
stained of gold;
light touches, without announcement, the dark,
and there lie about silver sighs.
And so, with care we employ the hand,
with regret know impropriety,
and with vigilance we offer prayers.

***

Let my back forget its straight leaning,
my shoulders to fold into softness,
and my arms and hands place
in prayerful laying. Cause ever, in
these moments my head to bow,
let the petals that cover the eyes of my thought,
but, more, of my heart, close into a
moment's repose and cleave to a
sweet peace of a short, dark season
where only friendly smoke and
brilliant stars move in dance around
the maiden moon,
her light not kept, but as chaste as
her jeweled belt and as her faithful key.

***

Can we be loved for the roses we grow,
brought into tender sentiment for tears caught by
our watch; touched in thought for the stones we lift
away, blessed for seeing inside the deep of another.

If so, then let me be alive, awake, to caress
the earth, reach for falling dark awareness, lift
away weights too heavy for others' given strength,
open my soul to the universe of all knowings and
unknowing—for in these beatitudes I find a self,
one that is as flowered companionable, gentle with
the hours, and comforting when seasons close.

***

"And I am left…"

The most worthy, endless circle that lies in the
path of existence touches me with
amazement, over, and over again:
as often as day and night are, the
exuberance and hope of morning, the stoic
will of endurance in day, the resignation
and acceptance in evening and night,
with its ever-promised spectacle
of new day—
over and over again, within the trappings
of mood, disappointment, fatigue,
and beleaguered hope—on, on, to
more of the pattern to be played out.
We mortals, lesser gods,
die, but rest immortal, that we do, for a
season, on these "golden, earthly
sands"—continue.

***

As—Rain Coming: to the dry dust of Elizabeth

—The chimes were beautiful, for they sounded
every striking of my heart, ever constant, as
the will of my heart,
truly as the words of my thoughts,
the flesh of my spirit.
—the dark was gentle, holding, as the new purpose
of my will, will to be lost in the dark's deep,
as my heart, if lost to such as a first.

—the wind moved as flowing water, as unseen love; leaping
flame, as voice to peace of struggle,
as its full joy of content,
as a mercy, peace the follows pain:
yet a night rainbow whose arc
falls into my receiving heart; embracing as
arms which hold all the tears of every
night before, bitter prologue to
a new scene, a painting of sound and
movement, images in thoughtful
quiet, sorrow's touch, impotent on a bed of hours,
my soul, within blessing,
calling out "Amen."

***

Magnolias are beginning to bloom again,
coming May, and anniversary of the fall—
I will always remember—death before
a life of wounding that has held secrets
of beauty, these to be chosen again, if this be the
only arrangement offered; this beauty and its dressing of
closer gold than yearnings for its touch, its
distance not to provide,
but these promising no
casting of shadow, more
the adolescent's secret

imaging, these
I know together, with
thanksgivings.

***

In close moments, we struggle and weep
over the bitter portion of our day;
and when offered us are beauty and good,
we sigh that these may not bloom into completion,
that they will, whole or part conclude.
Could we not our souls holding,
With almost reverential fear and gentleness,
in selected moments,
be transfused with the glory and bliss
our dreams have drawn for us.
Such would be a knowing,
Incomplete of war,
the blight and creeping of disease,
the cruel agony in wounds of the soul.
We could then spend our hours
on the far side of the mountain,
in resolution,
stitching clever and beautiful patterns,
or painting with colors of our reflected splendor,
our words and conversation
describing our moments of glory—
quietly content that our treasure is altogether within.
For we are living coals, unto fire,
to burst from our most inward and cavernous self,
even that within wandering skins,
into wonderful flame,
such as the paramour revealed to her lord,
to consume all of that dark and still,
to, with our ashes,
layer soul upon soul.

***

Easter Visit
2005

stay longer if you must,
but
come soon if you may;
whatever the complexion of
circumstance and sentiment,
hold me in your thoughts as
the road folds out, a ribbon of gathering anticipation,
before you.
Dark and shadow filled up the night,
but jeweled light found
corners in my heart, light
of laughter, wisdom, and care.
I am more when you are near me,
and this "more" I share, give back
to Thee;
stay longer if you must,
but come sooner if you may.

***

And when you are come to me,
love me if you can—if you will—
for beauty of my nourishment,
for Thou art bright and fair,
my wisdom, my heart's strength and glory.

***

If the tangled nest of pain can lift
the fledgling new, and so to
greet with joy, until moments collected
when the poor corpus, fatigued of
natural insults in birthings
demanding travail,
mummers, that the coming new

leave its clay to
lift away,
beyond temporal recognition,
in purist spirit, freed—
—Careful—must hurt find its gallantry;
for noblest death is, yet,
that most without,
in the light we know,
Most,
To be the day.

***

The Pronouncement

I am sad when I consider how old my brothers are;
I imagine, in truth know,
that I am as an onion conceit
with layers of fretful feelings,
righteous and humble,
with the always attending pain,
the heart molten rock
that has not yet bled in completeness.
My swallows are hurried and deep;
my breath is almost a sacred burden,
precious and heavy.
And the passing of time is like a pronouncement
that we are, in every instance,
steps toward conclusion
which we forever look beyond,
to pine
that there be for us to know
eternity's leaf and snowfall.

***

Winter Highwayman
A. Noyes/Elizabeth

A cold winder came in the night,
blowing, blowing, into the midnight
hour,
through my south pines, or so it seemed;
and their voices were like great fans, in the
wind,
blowing, blowing, weeping
above the last insect chorus, bringing
memory, as itself a wind,
making sounding fans, crying in
my heart,
my consciousness of time,
of summer passed, of season and change,
of loss:
and I reached to the spent runner of autumn,
that I catch the baton, to press toward
rest on the bed of winter.

***

My thoughts run all the way out,
and are as full as all
eternity, full and heavy with leanings
that is freeing somewhat, but bending more, still;
for my heart is empty in small and
large portions, weeping for its lost parts. And
there is tension, struggle, ready jousting,
as the bull brute before its fate with the
beautiful matador.
How high my thoughts that stand fully dressed,
to take the primitive. It will be midst
weeping, for I am in love with
all my thought; it is first, irony past
justice

that only I know them and am the one
sacrifice to them.
When I lie in repose, in thought, whether in
feigned laughter, games, conversation or quiet
industries,
no one will see the ashen hue, the limpid
shroud,
the full finality, for I die daily, a familiar
sport, to begin again.
True repose will be a surprise, but a knowing
surprise.
Brown leaves, dry and featherlike, lie below
absent moths which, in their close
recency,
bejeweled my lighted chime, whose, its voice,
wept the passing.

***

O day, how joyful to know, but with what grief. Also, to know,
dewdrops hanging about, waiting their glory,
monuments to love about my rose—
difficult this matter of beauty,
reminding, exacting, hewing,
honorable pain.

***

If I could say just once,
walk through just once—
but I fall away and search out
all the back doors, the softer words,
glance through a window—
and wait—
the agonized state of the uncertain,
of the small of strength, the
intensely feeling beside its broken part.
Could faith, could fact, could company ride in

on Olympian chariots to rescue, they would fail,
for I do not, as much as I, in full strife,
wish to do so, yet do not want to break my true
silence, for it is the breath in my soul;
and to open it to voice would leave me unclasped,
but more, my familiar pain departed, empty.
Do I cherish, am I enamored of my pathos: it
ebbs and flows, and in that movement are
small reprieves, moments of brief relief,
time to step back and question the merit
of disclosure, but the in-between steps almost
walk me into the deep where I cannot breathe—
to decision or decided ambivalence.
Perhaps this unfortunate portion, without a horse,
is the piece I wish for myself—no willed
regret, or hurt; quiet, none.
Time came round to something at last
finding a happening; I had writhed
and turned to and about, and
then, as seasons must, poised, as a
ballerina to execute, waited until
the lateness was such that the horse
would have made no difference.

Is this script really mine or am I simply jousting with ideas;
I have seldom left matters to this point.
I raise my hands to Thee; Holy Presence.

***

Canto Five

But oh inside fire, you spring in all beauty,
into certain manifestings, and I cannot
know, ever, into now, in
reflection,
that it is true that I will find warmth,
in dressings and voice I cannot
now find,
but light water giving first love's weight,
heavy understanding where it has not
been the octane of ashes;
instead, found is uninvited wisdom, gentle fire
whose flame must be, is, peace.

***

One

I am going into the night,
and the new blade of January grass
will be dark;
it will grow in long hours of rest,
and I, as the blade, will rise presently
to stand taller, greener, stronger.
Oh, my soul,
bear me up through until morning,
for the pain in darkness
will be my nourishment.
A good day with sadness in the backrooms.

***

Two

I am in the belly of the night,
having descended into the ever familiar
"little death,"
And I struggle inside a silent consciousness,
the silent pain of spiritual knowing;
if the obvious were not so,
that day is, even now, quietly, patiently
pushing into the dark,
my soul's lonely song would sigh
and perish.

***

Complexioned Against

Oh, let me now know all that I can,
that I have known, that I do know,
not to bring back the sunset,
eyes in innocent, bright expectancy,
haloed of soft, becoming
masculine laughter, the chronicle,
ever often repeated, of the
virginal sweet olive—
these all, as billowing white clouds into beautiful passing,
dreams of old men, those not ever lost
from their youth, wounding
in this very truth, but will, complexioned against, the sword
not to ever strike true, but to be left, given over to its sweet repeating.
the kingdom fell into decay long ago,
and out the teapot,
the wandering is long—
The Way of the Pilgrim—

***

a long, reflective day, with backward glances, overmuch—
diminishing, continuing—
And when the yearning grows
heavier than its
bearing,
then the night of earth
and soul falls deeply into
its hours.
The house of feeling is racked by
winds of sentiment,
and respite seems beyond the full
of darkness.
Ought left is to but know that pain
finds beauty,
andso, in radiant glory, we will, in time,
stand.
In soft, shy rainfall, with weighted thought and
feeling—
Ah, raindrops, innocent pearls of clarity
true, fall freely, fully this time, that I not be
reminded, enjoined again to this
wealth of pain.
In the amen of quieted, ringing bells—

***

Epilogue

Perhaps it is only that I spin and weave,
and so, heavily with metaphor and conceit,
the conclusion being merely a matter of conjecture
I know that this matter of the conclusion
is fearful to me,
but I am also hopeful;
I hope with a prejudiced certitude
that as the brown and golden leaves fall,

to dance and play in the wind and sunlight,
to be seen and recognized by a patient wanderer—
in like fashion I will move in the wind and sunlight
and I will be known to him who stops
to touch a leaf
and finds, indeed, my soul.

***

When the moments pass in grey procession,
I choose sometimes to leave my dish for the morning,
to wash,
that there be purpose to my rising.
I glance often toward it
and know that I have thought and chosen,
and that I stand;
sweetness cushions effort,
and struggle becomes the bloom of faith;
purest moonlight is left in the morning's dew,
in the face of the spider's lace.
The poignant beauty in the night's record
will offer salutation to the day and
the circle of night closes with small tiles of hope
whose patterns find the morning;
we will then ride the ribbon of the sun
as a fine mermaid on her sea beast,
to know, in patience
the wealth in the small grandeur of the dragon fly.

***

The beautiful prologue seems distant to me, now,
the waiting, the trumpeting of your voice in
receiving, speaking my name; the unseen capture
of our first glance to each other—and the first touch,
in passing or with press.
I miss, in these moments, our laughter together,
the wit, poor and better, the verses and narratives;
I am without the food of the promises in your eyes,

the billowing up of expectations out the progress
of close and sweet, yet passionate conversation.
You are joy to me, all good to me, and presently,
in these recent days, I have been empty of Thee:
ought else to say of these in each other, your
sensually intense, your incredibly tender, blessing.

***

Keepsake

Come back to me moments,
hours, present days of expectancy, promise,
joy imagined:
these sustaining avenues of
blessed hope,
yesterday's feeding nourishment,
today's tomorrow's dreams.

***

In the storm scene painting,
I want my clouds to be while daisies
with happy centers, perhaps of
sunset hues,
to billow up above the darkened
water, as celestial beings,
lifting off my person, to carry me into,
between the blue-grey clouds,
to the higher vault of azure blue where light
reigns true, and there are not
reminders
of forecast rain.
Thinking of painting begun during the night
of intermittent sleep—
I want it to be day; I have not yet stepped through.
American Beauty
Lily

***

... comrade to quieted, and many musings,
now with, always, greater haste in reachings
toward fullest knowing, finding that
in them, these, true imaginings, rest my truest loves, in the
very hands of He, my keeper, HolyfatherGod,
ever, of all my seasons, these terrestrial,
even into afterglow, and those in, perhaps,
the darkened eternal.

Sunday morning, just noon, grey day, feeling
poorly, hands, fatigue, lost.
Birds' cries, not the hawk, and why do I note; he of Richard,
my poor lost Richard, he of none, gone now ten years since
his last glimpse, in poor afternoon sunlight, his grapevine in
its last, to him, September.

***

Winter is come, cold and hard,
the winter of yesterday's stall and its
emptiness, its glaring bare
to warm the winter horse.
Winter is come when the leaves left of yesterday
blow into somewhere, ragged and torn,
wretched vestiges of a radiance
of greens, now alive only in recollection.
Winter is come so that passersby, in frigid
haste, move like the leaves, cold like
the horse, into somewhere warm.
Winter is come like an unpleasant breath,
moving against our sweeter selves,

reminding the paradox of seasons,
to be simply borne, to live with empty
and bare, grey and dim, knowing
there is a scape beneath, resting, breathing,
growing, to push out, its heart
instinctually strong, housing an ancient
devotion to self-dressing in the
rest of need to respond in the impatient above.

***

I wish only in these such moments,
a blessing, if but passing,
that within these extended stills,
the hued dark into which I would color,
into ever, magnanimously ported
outside circumstance and will.
Those comforts it may provide to my poverties:
to draw and erase, to hold and await,
until light, its can being the greatest
pathos we ought ever,
but to never know or bear,
its unkindnesses, in fading that
within the dark,
to arrive,
the blasphemy it can.

***

—Surely to hold in more than memory,
the great palace of yesterday, its
fatigue, now so long with me,
to be put into a ditch to die—
a new antidote, if only mercy in
nothingness,
that of letting go.
Let the dream of the day lift up, away,
leaving nothing, for nothing
is, and does not need be borne.
Oh, to be a penguin, all in one, together
knitted into one, no plan of
separation, trying to find, somehow—
Where, when, the golden thread of light to sew me
together, with a needle surely
of flowing blood,
my humanity, somehow, must—

I have about me, flowing over
and around me, a silk
of brightest hued happiness,
laughter, near ecstasy at moments
of special beauty;
but the silk slips always away,
quickly,
lost in the moment, caught
and realized,
its mundanity, its wretchedness
beside its noblesse,
its cars and windows carrying
all away into the distance.

***

If I drop the blade on all
their heads, what I see, but
more, feel, their drawing
out of me my very crimson—
what so: I am alone in this moment just
as I would be alone after the blood.
Curtsies forgotten, indignities touted,
how with glee some
hold their bags of touch and thought,
glances aside, attendance to task with
an appropriate farewell, more than
drew the salutation.
No one cares in thoughtful leanings
except in the arrangement of his rooms,
or if on the outside of his rooms, robes and
belts, buckles and hat pins catch
the prize.
Oh better be the blade strike my neck than
others, for I cannot arrange ought of
them, and of me, my eyes can close
to all manner of dying.

***

Without fancy, or more somber thought,
sitting at the feet of matron
greens,
and looking upward to a wide bowl
of slightest blue, filled to its portion,
the morning takes on the nature of a
fair ribbon, with stones of lovely blinking, counterpointed colors,
a ribbon that stretches out to become
the day.

Sweetness overmuch would pour out this
scene, this vessel of reality's finest
nectar, but more, a golden mead that
fills and offers, yet, pleasure past its
sweetness.

***

To watch the night come in is to
see a beauty die;
light awakens, in finding,
catching, enhancing, by making golden
music.
And when shadows begin their slow
predatory engulfing, the gold in the
music
takes on a tarnish, dressing with a passing,
groomed by farewelling.
O night,
if thy coming, must, gather the
remnants of the day, the
small, apologetic smiles of light,
and bless them
with thy silver, hurriedly, quickly,
that the dark Rose of midnight give her
kiss of death to saying darkness,
her kiss of life to promising, coming
again,
truest beauty and light.

***

I wish no more the left,
nor, in sanguine guise, bear until the
morn;
like used Santiago after his fish, I wish only
to sleep the dreams
of my mountain.
And—taste, if all is kind, the
confections of Creekside violets,
fresh, as in memory's dew;
to know imbuement of maiden buds,
blest of the noblesse,
and die,
leaving to the hindward, in its relegated
place,
the fabled unknown, its press and angst,
its museum smile of insistent,
if quiet, invitation.

***

Left Only

All seems done, left only with into
denouement, toward conclusion;
the smile begun in the east is quieted to
the west; trumpets do not now
appoint the organ,
and breasts, in firstness,
high and firm,
hang, in awkward loveliness,
as fruit, spent with the warmth of great hours.
Its own solitude hears the clock continue,
speaking each moment's
farewelling,

and with these fallen hours, a new day
will in,
but to find I, Elizabeth, contemplating
crossed arms and legs,
for the sword is at my neck,
and its dragon-master wears a cape of black.
To say goodbye to the pomegranate, showing
in its rare purity, the organ,
grand,
in procession, to the ritual of the lock promising
new day—to say goodbye is difficult, wielding
herein the sting, in this night of "little death."

***

Nearly full light, ivory
under shadow that will lift
away into the innocent
beauty of expectant sunrise—
property only of southern
springs, Mississippi,
particularly—to listen
to the far-away loveliness of the
entering mourning dove—
oh, my heart, can fullness know
all of inside to fill up the
greater scape of all otherness.

***

Come see, come see,
I am, I am me;
I have been touched, and gently,
and I can touch, gently.
I know the eternity in the hurt
of a fading moment;

the matter of tenderness is
smaller,
almost a Sarto balance,
but yet a hard knot,
a stone that does not
move.
And so,
Come see, come see,
I am, I am me;
I have been touched, gently,
and I can touch, gently.
Within my rhapsody is the
hard knot,
but all around the knot plays
the rhapsody.

***

The Purpose

They come to stand in silver cold,
moonlit blossoms on stems in shadow,
pressed together.
Theirs will be a dark radiance,
fire within the ebony cloak of night,
their colors taken into the chilling breath of March:
if with beauty,
to transport and sit on the windowsill,
within the evening's moonfall;
and with its falling lost,
to sit in passing death,
until the blessing light of day
when their beauty grace exclaims,
in jocund words,
their purpose joyful.

***

Rose Rose Thoughts

It is in the secret chambers of my own, yet
singular, place, whether closet,
inside, or thicket, outside,
that I open my heart—most to my personal
cognizance—that I reveal—of my first being,
and some colorings of others—through
metamorphic structure and description which
draws, undresses, embellishes—together with unhappy shadows.
Petaled dust, now, here, alone of others—in quieted
light, together with an accepted self—only
reminds summer warm rose in a time when the
property, or quality of perfect form
appears in the forgotten light of evening, the several years
sculpted by their comments of softest touch:
the soft petals of rose Rose.
They had come together as dust, with the dance of
natural law, but touched by my glance, spoke a beautifully
prepared verse of love, lost, in tender
revelation.

Early evening, with thoughts of R

***

Proverb

All of our shouts,
our mummerings,
are but begging compositions,
that we be recognized in our spirits,
that the moonfire anoint us,
the day's star embolden us that we be known.
We wish most,
of all,
that we be known,
to then be joined to our beginning part.

And so, of it all,
there is but a journey of days
that becomes in their fullness,
the richly tinted,
fragranced breath of prayer.

***

"I Wish a Rose"

If I could love, again, truly,
the pushing down of all the years,
and, before, the senseless hope,
these would flower up, into a joy,
a completeness,
that even Cinderella, an innocent sweetheart,
could not image—
nor the seasoned matron know
the inside of it,
so that her hand would catch to her throat.
If I could love, again, truly,
I would not spar concerning the moment,
but forgive the clock, the night, the seasons,
to only be fulfilled in the knowing.
Though more queenly than kingly, I may wear
two bodices to hide my
tremulous heart, but I would forget all,
forgive all, and conquer every dissonance,
that I may experience this exquisite all.

remembering, long time away, tonight, and the many layers of protection
from every adversity, and counting my holdings,
finding nothing—what price glory—I have saved
myself into emptiness, and am not
confident that I can make the walk back—

Certainly the Rose is the only flower; andso, in this moment, I wish a Rose.
And it lives more than a moment, so that a troth is must to be fashioned; still,

I wish a Rose. When I awaken, all may appear a dream, a riddle, a fable, but my scripted sentiments let me know that my heart, in all of its turns, has prepared me, able—And I, yet, wish a Rose.

***

Vaporous Yo-yo, Two

I am back to my old self
(at least the more pleasant self), today;
following close in thought, however, is the
arrangement of hours
in yesterday.
I am, now, often, the older, earlier yo-yo,
mercurial to the extent of exhaustion.
What demons are loosed again, what manner
of vapors rise up about me.
I complain, in anger, and weep into
repenting;
I have my dolls and medicinal wisdom, but, yet,
so tenuous holds my flesh,
my spirit.
resting, assessing in dissonance and despair—

There are those who love me, but they will come
not to love me; such is my poor histoire.

I will sit, again, with Sappho when the winter comes:
cold and alone, again.

***

our becoming
it sang again, an evening song,
brownskins and swallows, inside
rainbows and faithful hymns;
then became, out of resting,
a pasture of innocence in which
I walked, raising my hands
to catch feathered and devotional hues.
The wealth time adds to experience became
as adventure of
the far meadow,
the cool of the evening as a laying
on of hands, a blessing of
good, kept,
a silver pearl, or perhaps a grateful
tear
shining in early summer moonlight.

***

Two Images

My thought bears the weight
of the disc,
collecting all of its being,
just before lifting to
freedom.
And in the fellowship of thought,
comes, not, the image
of early morning—
the heavy lifting, slowly, slowly,
of the moon, full, fair, of the noblesse, through
a giving window,

but with practiced certainty, into its down.
"The moon is down," and
thought wings, the lark in its
effetely being, self—how else to find new day, but so given into the
presence of self, out heaviness and prescribed
law—into the beauty of openness,
movement: joyful being.

recalling two images in these breakfast hours, as the sun spreads its
glory into the all of day: the disc near midnight, when effort at
sleep was great, and later, several hours, at glancing
out, to see the lifting of the moon into the away—

The world of the Natural sings always to me, my constant keeper
of beauty, and truth—not at all judgmental, but as much
so, real.

***

The bamboo and the butterfly
came to me in summer's
beginning closing:
together, in grace and peaceful movement,
their only adventure, beauty,
but
the beauty gathered is of pastels
about richest hues so that
there emerges, in a waltz-like
manner,
accompanied by a thoughtful wind,
a monarch's salad—and
a sudden splash of tiny multicolored,
perfectly geometrically arranged
veins
that wing up and out, in joy, to the
waiting sky.

***

If you must go, wait until night,
so that it will be night.
Guide our souls into the more together,

the intimacy of moving, or standing
light;
and let our bodies joyfully carry
them into the flower of one, each to the other.

Her cheek to his chest,
his hand to her waist;
rapture whose sensual
reach awakens souls in deep repose
to rise in flight,
coming together in a past that
rivals the touch of meadow mists
in early morning.

**

Driving in Sabbath warm, of a new summer
prologue's finishing lines; seeing,
on looking up, into the
wide of blue, decorated with wandering
white whispers
a tree came forward, to me, a tree, grande,
and wind caught it so that,
as a woman to her lover, its limbs unfolded
with a tremor of excitement into a
resting of rippling and relaxing, to graceful
movements of trust and deep caring.
Sitting at prayers, before service, and close to its
center, the mornings light spilled out into
each portion of the altar's stained glass,
it becoming a sensual, as a spiritual
touching,

for all the readings, prayers, and hymnody,
spoke of "all together"; "coming together";
and "as one"; and I felt to weep, so real
was the marriage of soul and corpus,
giftings divine, as should to be; and at
the image of thee, come to my inward
eye, in this all, I came to weep,
freely; I felt my tears brought me close
to saintliness, since there was, in
these tears, in these beautifully caught
moments, and in their recounting—
found were gentle healings, into the grail of fullness
and wholeness.

***

Mortality is a silently raging cancer, the
ever malignant reality—before, but borne
from first awareness, whether in noise or
quiet, in movement or still, yet in laughter
or weeping.
It images in selected moments and hours,
of pensive postures, or in dramatic events
dressed of varied colors and feeling, yet in
seasons of soft reverie and darkened fancy.
Knowing or closeted, it, in insidiously clever

burking of supportive breath, takes away, even
itself, into our absence.

***

Ever-Marlin

The sun is fierce in its constancy
of movement, incomprehensible haste
in rising toward falling;
and to hold its glory is to run,
to lean into its present light,
grasping, catching hopefully, its beautiful rage in burning
together, forcing apart shadow,
the music of childhood fancies that
the existential shark tied to our skiff at days' end,
will somehow,
through prayer and purity,
or the smoky finesse of the
seasoned gambler, the found lost thought
of the faithful philosopher,
the gentleness of the cotter,
it, somehow, to be received
a marlin.

***

I raised the door, and cold rushed in,
much as the Easter storm,
and I knew, again, perhaps with
the greatest, most poignant
sign, that in a season, my old man, who
brought, through my hesitancy,
my fear of it, the spring that I had felt was
lost, to many
seasons, to many of
everything, lost but redeemed,
lost out his arms,
now, but in a hurting gratitude,
found into the always left me.

***

When the unrestrained, constant singing
from insects of night has died into
a newly lost season;
when flowers struggle with their
remaining glory's radiance;
when woven into the natural face are
feigned smiles and circumstances that fill
as forebodings—
when these, then—shadows of a gloom not
real, not yet, are known in the heart
as true prologue to dark—

The evening is still, the climes quiet; shadows
remind hours to be visited before the
crystal pieces will spread forth
their beauty again.
Where are the good times, the safe times,
those of kin and friend, true—and dear:
they have left with the season, for thought
wanders into autumn and winter, finding lost
what once was held: deep, radiant certainty
of the day, and those in it, the hour, surely, the beauty
of the moment.

To grow is to reach, to break the bindings that
are part of each, our circumstance;
in these movements is the feast of day, the
sanctuary of night, but after the season
of green meadows and bright berries, reaching
and bindings having become mixed, some the bittersweet
record, sunset and twilight are acknowledged;
and we fancy that perhaps the old paths might have,
truly, held the better feast, that we must
gather what trappings of those that are left to
secure us in the, now, night.

***

Today's Leaves

Drifting downwards, moving along
paths in warm winds, blown
over the once absolute
verdant green
of spring, into the matron shades
of summer,
—leaves laughed out to me, and smiled
in natural silences.
Watermarks became lines, and
broken tissue spread out crinkles
above and around
lighter colorations against those
darker.
And faces, their soul portals, arranged
around the tenuous circle of self
to call to me, that I cross
over, to embrace these, nature's
manifestations of my soul's
yearnings and reaching.
I crushed them in hands as holding, more,
caressing, a reverence, as close to
my heart as I might, their
pieces falling away as I embraced.

***

A brief visitation made its farewelling,
descending
with my weeping, but I had been, was
with them, in my fashion,
and my pattern is mine,
past knowing and the brooding scholar's
reason toward wisdom.

***

I need no creed, not liturgy, only the kind
needs I, and others, seek to bring
Holy Presence closer to us.
Let rules, and edicts, let feast days, and
humble behaviors find their place,
knowing, those pleasing with them
that they are but our little signals,
our rainbows and snowflakes
to Presence gathering in our hearts.
Most, in silence, bejeweled solitude, is
Presence in our hearts: decisions, hurt
and loss, guilt beside regret, and
joy and thanksgivings—as the
laughter of my little brownskins,
prayerfully felt, true God, my God, inside
my heart.
The particulars must be left
to us in the still thoughts surrounding
the warm, spontaneous, innocent
laughter.

At a point at which I know only that I do not know.
I reason and listen to the laughter.

And I, in great tearfulness, come to this juncture.

Peace is just outside my door, to lead me into
this night and all of those left on this side and those
waiting on the far side.

***

In finished meaning, I find a great perplexity, a dissonance,
for I, into the mirror of existence, find myself paradoxical;
the snows of yesteryear fall in inundation over me, and
within the same, I cannot, with the complete of my strength,
ableness, wish—I cannot embrace the present moment, the
whole of it, its gold of harvest.
Adding season and circumstance, beside will, the riddle

might finesse relief by escaping to the fire in the given
bramble, to find, moth-like loveliness, in easy manipulation
of the intended, clandestine embrace of the dark lover, ever the heart
of the flame, offering finality and cessation of struggle.

To begin is difficult, to conclude is difficult, and each morning
bright brings this eternal dilemma; when in it, beauty is drained
off into the unattainable away, and energy to find it again, more,
Voila—why, then, not the whore-like surrender, which, like a man
lighting a woman's cigarette, a like inverted coitus, we may usurp,
if without noblesse, the pattern and enjoy the ultimate power of
control when dependence, and confused weakness can no longer
weep impotently into our portioned divinity.

Suicide is an enjoyable, thoughtful fancy, it, intermittently
giving me relief that I, if stubbornly, have choice with
what was never choice: in sum, it is a shadowed game I
often play—

***

After Small Sleep

Day, O day—I am together with praise as the
mystic dervish such that I am, into your lighted
mists, passed with the dark; this day, the hand,
full of dream songs opened, letting their liftings
ariel toward the eternal away.
Beautiful malaise, requiring potions and powders,
salts of fragrance, pungent, true, stolen glimpses
through opened windows—
a dragonfly wing in its lighted moment—a face given
to time, to be borne away on constant winds, wandering
winds, perhaps even lost winds.

***

Fullness is goodly measured by its becoming emptiness;
modest and to the aside smiles, as buds, too small and
pale to flower, are not remembered in their absence, as sweet as
these could be when they began their journeys.
My music unheard, as my words, my strength expressed
to others, or the greater wide, as unmanifest—as worthy as
they purposed to be, will evoke no tears in my silence.
Would a rainbow, without raindrops, could a soul without
tears—could, no—if hearts do not need their presence;
they are, in truth, denied, rendered empty, not even ever
a loss.
Need not to bring a drape for the light, for it bloomed within
itself, alone, not to illuminate more than, perhaps, a
question and dismissal.

***

These my words,
my secret,
closeted images:
these layer down into my soul,
the whole of which is the corner and my darkness.
In that hallowed portion of ourselves that is feeling—
knowing, sensing—
finding holds the very essence of being,
and playing out is only shadow inside a season, not
the eternal song of the ever self.

Elizabeth

CONCLUSION

There is a modest line from an old comic character, familiar to almost everyone, which states a major portion of the thesis now presented: Popeye's statement, "I y'am what I y'am"— insistently—with a personal struggle in it. Within its flowering in the sixties over the world, and in this country, this statement's sentiment has become the credo of the remainder of history into today: greater than the opening of the eastern sphere, the occurrence of the Renaissance, the embracing of the wide of space; and somehow matters have arranged so that this personal self (the "I," "me") must be acknowledged and to some degree, in some fashion, accepted—to be reflected back to the seeking self as a nearly "without flaw" personal identity. A player, alone, too often may find, as Tolstoy remarks "disorder and early sorrow." The arrangement is never just of one—always, at the least, two or unhappiness finds exchanges which lack fulfillment. Our lives are, most, a search for peace, after birth, until death, whatever, however, it be accomplished, probably by showing our need to some "accepting enough" entity.

The pursued in the verse "The Hound of Heaven" by the devotional British poet Francis Thompson exemplifies each of us as we mature in our steps:

> Ah Fondest, Blindest, weakest,
> I am He whom Thou seekest.
> Thou dravest love from thee
> who dravest me.

We may or may not be aware, for insight is difficult; it involves truth and acceptance, and ideally, redemption or "turning around." Name, station, personal qualities—these are not so much the important ingredients, but rather ability, perception and intuitiveness. Some simply have a less difficult altercation with reality than others, not an awakening, a "catastrophic," one, but in the general, recognizing that accepting objective reality lies at the apex of all the activity of the self.

The lock, then, can be loosed and the variety of the happening of this event is great, but the kept chest can be opened. The magnitude of such action can be greater than ordinary description. The pain and joy, the revelations, the reflection, the taking into and acceptance—such is the life examined, if not explained. Truth found in this venture, whether by one's own perusal of himself, a deep prayer life, the guidance of a professional—whatever method is chosen, it is opening and looking at one's heart—the pathotic epitome, the vinegar and the thorns within the crown of being.

There is no formula for "an individual": we know certain wisdoms which add to the happy or unhappy soul, everything from genetic factors to unhappy separation anxiety, but we cannot know just how to arrange peace. It includes an absence of strife, of sparing—of pain and the opportunity to embrace the beautiful and good. We each find our way, and looking back we speculate as the curious, the grateful, the spent in gathering, the disappointed, the fulfilled in all manner in kinds—and man is a very special creature who must have his individuality—even, quiet, in his chest closed into open. "I am that I am"—God on Mt. Horeb to Abraham; the only difference with Popeye's statement is a relative pronoun; God and man are matters out the expression of their hearts.

God is, in a sense, all, a concept whose being became a gradual consensus of major thinkers/ seekers over many years, and we yet cannot begin to understand the largess of all the thought brought to it—possibly, by …resonating similar sentiments: that we are alive, and breathe and think—that we are surrounded by life—this reality is God, in us, in all.

A similar statement alongside that of Popeye's, "all I am is all I have," can be given thought—a paraphrased blues statement. We are, with or without examination, acceptance, peace—that we are, comprised of genetic components, dressed by outside factors such as social norms and expectations, instruction, and experience. We are still, must have, others: our individuality, be it known or not, or divinely directed, our actions form the gestalt of each soul's work, our message, our song, as stated in a variety of verses by the early modern American poet Walt Whitman, known even today through his fresh openness of self—and his acceptance in it. Our must adhering to certain particulars of the "charade" does not destroy the real self completely. It may leave unfulfillment, remorse and reaching, but we are who we are and for those fortunate, the chest, if unhappily closed by silence, can be opened to become a grail to seek through chosen expression.

I am no different from most and so I speak for us all: if these words can be of help—comfort, direction, usable morsels of truth, strength of recognition of the power of will inside grace—then be so: I cannot say that I understand or know, for I do not; I can say that I believe because I feel.

Elizabeth
April 30, 2017
In deepest night

CONCLUSIVE ASIDE

All matters that are, that have stepped through the dusts of time, and hold delightful expectancies for future hours—these each, all, inclusively must begin. Beginnings color, suggest, and in great fashion, draw boundaries in their steps along the way—and they cast their shadowed glow about at the close. Such is sweet and such is sad, but it is a reality played out in every instance of life, without exception.

At times, the colorings arrive in lovely attire, suggestions of fine wines with condiments, all of the good and true; in others, such is not so—but rather include a larger portion of "vinegar and thorns," the passion always must to be played out in a very personal fashion.

In the verse narrative of...*Agatha Moi*, as the beginnings at once balanced negatively alongside a coloring of an abundance of beauty—and the full scape opened to be seen through eyes wide to perceive the whole, a dissonance arranged not ever completely resolved. The "everything" achieved is a metaphorical surmising, allowing comfort, productivity, and most, hope.

Elizabeth
June 30, 2017, 11:00 p.m.

Works by Elizabeth Clayton

I, Elizabeth
2007

Songs from the Eleventh Month
2008

A Thousand White Gardenias
2009

Unto Relationship
2009

Musings
2009

La Libelule
2010

Chanson de Harold
2011

Shenandoah Songs
2012

The Sun and Geranium Poems
2012

Scarlet Flow
2012

Seasonal Portions
2013

The Myth of Being
2015

The Quiet Sheba Trilogy
2014-2016

We Lesser Gods
2016

We Lesser Gods Addendum
2016

In Springtime's Fields of Glory
2016

Short Harvest
2017

Devotions in Elizabeth House
2017

I have spoken true…and I have pleased…and stars dress me.
I will not reach for the sun and moon.

Agatha Moi is a long-thought, very full bramble of ruminations of a life through which struggle enabled the sacrament of a kind of purification—a cleanliness of negativism, fear, and doubt, the redressing of fear, and the pathos of understanding the loss of, most, beauty—into an acceptance of an argument aspiring which became, finally, truly, unnecessary.

"Wearing" can prove difficult, as the verse narrative demonstrates, but using its reality of studied perception with the "forward appendage of thought—hope"—a cathartic quest has offered a medium, a fashion after the grail: one of truths, beauty and acceptance without regret.

If wisdom be found through example, perhaps we may look into ourselves to accept and trust, if with questions, the spirit waiting there to be unveiled, to not be in reactive discovery, challenged, or filled of questions yet thought found unworthy. Growth can occur within the rooms of doubt, as with examination, casting off, reaffirming, or finding new alternatives, but we must be wise in the thoughtful simplicity of a behavior truly no more than rearranging—replacing an acceptable portion of truth in the portion left empty—that we not be found, "left waiting," without our "stars" to dress our "person."

About the Author

Elizabeth Clayton began teaching at the age of twenty at the University of Southern Mississippi. Presently retired, she is spending her days reviewing and preparing her works for publication. Clayton has published eighteen works (primarily poetry) since the release of her autobiography in 2007, which chronicles her struggles with bipolar disorder. In November 2012, she was inducted into the Literary Hall of Fame, Sigma Kappa Delta, and nominated for the Eric Hoffer award by her publisher in early spring 2013. She is also featured in the summer 2013 quarter of *Forward Magazine*, and her work, *Scarlet Flow*, was shown in the World Book fair in London, England in early 2013, receiving the Golden Seal of Excellence Award in 2014, following.

Additionally, on January 5 and February 9, 2014, she was featured in the *New York Times* "New Voices, New Perspectives" segment; her most recent work, *Quiet Sheba*, a trilogy, begun in 2015 was completed (two final volumes) in February 2016. For this work, she received the Golden Seal of Excellence Award from her publisher. More recently, her latest work, *We Lesser Gods*, was published in late summer 2016, its addendum receiving the Golden Seal of Excellence Award in summer 2017.